SHOOTING IN THE DARK

Bolt and Tom had been up before dawn, riding the rough trail all day in order to make Angel's camp before dark. Persistence had paid off. They reached the camp two hours ahead of schedule. But now, Bolt's muscles were paying him back for the demands of the hard ride.

Despite his intention to sleep lightly with one ear tuned to his door, Bolt fell into a deep sleep minutes after his head hit the bed.

Sometime in the middle of the night, Bolt awoke with a start. He felt his mattress jiggle and knew someone was at his bedside. His hand shot up to his gunbelt. He felt the bed move again with the weight of the intruder.

Frantic, Bolt fumbled in the dark for his pistol.

"Don't worry. It's just me," whispered a voice.

It was a woman's voice, soft and husky. . . .

#11
BOLT

THE LAST BORDELLO
BY CORT MARTIN

ZEBRA BOOKS
KENSINGTON PUBLISHING CORP.

ZEBRA BOOKS

are published by

KENSINGTON PUBLISHING CORP.
475 Park Avenue South
New York, N.Y. 10016

Printed in the United States of America

Chapter One

The two riders, trail-weary as they rode into Angel's Camp, reined up on a scene of madness.

People rushed toward the center of the clapboard town from all directions, pushing, yelling, jostling, stumbling, running as if to a fire.

Bolt, the tall man on the big bay stud, reached down, grabbed a man by the coat collar, stopped him in his tracks.

"What's going on here?" he asked.

"You'll see! Just let me go, mister, I don't want to miss this."

Bolt released his grip, looked at his companion.

"You smell something, Tom?" he asked.

Tom Penrod, the lanky man on the sorrel gelding, stretched up tall in the saddle, adjusted his Stetson over his tousled light brown hair. He threw his head back, sniffed the air.

"Tar. You reckon they're going to tar a roof?"

"Like hell. More likely a scoundrel. You got a short memory, friend."

Tom Penrod grinned weakly. The two men had encountered rails before and the smell of hot tar was not unfamiliar to them. More than once during their years on the cattle trails, they had witnessed the ritual of a rogue being tarred and feathered, a barbaric ceremony often reserved for the villain who was caught in bed with another man's wife.

A man rushing by them stumbled, fell near Bolt's horse. He looked up at the two dusty-faced strangers.

"You better hurry, boys. They're fixin' to tar and feather one of them harlots."

Bolt's face hardened. His eyes narrowed and a cloud shadow seemed to darken his features.

"That how you treat women in this town?" he asked, a bitter accusation tingeing his words.

"Cal Rader, he means to clean up Angel's Camp." The man got up, without bothering to dust himself off, and raced headlong into the pack of men and women scurrying toward a location around the corner of the next street.

Bolt touched spurs to his horse's flank. The bay jumped, broke into a gallop. Penrod lashed his reins over his horse's rump, tried to catch up. As they rode, the two men scattered the crowd, turned the corner.

The smell of tar was strong in their nostrils.

The din of people yelling, jostling for position, drowned out the sound of hoofbeats.

The mob was thickest in front of the Dry Creek Saloon, next to the Angels Hotel. Bolt rode right into them, right through the curses and threats, scattering men and women right and left. Tom followed the opening path and hauled up behind the bay stud.

The horses shied at the big smoke-blackened kettle

6

that boiled angrily atop a blazing fire in the street. Near the fire, a pair of men ripped pillows open, filled a washtub with musty chicken feathers. A group of men on the porch of the Dry Creek Saloon eyed the two riders. Two of them struggled with the girl they held between them.

"Let me alone!" she shrieked.

Sybil Childs looked to be no more than eighteen. Long strands of her blonde hair straggled down her rosy cheeks. She kicked one of the men, tried to bite another. They wrestled her out of range.

Bolt heard the sound of cloth ripping and saw one of the girl's breasts, creamy and soft, pour out of her bodice.

"Shut up, girl!" said a tall man on the porch, stepping in front of her. He ignored the two strangers on horseback, cleared his throat.

"Who's that?" asked Penrod of a spectator.

"Calvin Rader, pilgrim, and he's the big gun here. This here's a duly organized meetin' of the Merchant's Association."

"Looks more like a goddamned lynch party to me," muttered Penrod. "Who are the two galoots strong-arming the little lady?"

"Dave Talbot on the left, Pete Booker on the right. Good citizens, doing what's needed to clean up this town."

Bolt was silent, grim-faced. His jaw twitched as he memorized the faces of the men holding the girl.

"Listen up, everyone," bellowed Rader. He was a tall man, muscular, with dark brown hair, dark eyes, a razor scar across one high cheekbone. His mouth was curled, the lips thin under an even thinner moustache.

7

He wore a pin-striped suit, a clean Stetson, polished boots. He wore his pearl-handled pistol high and a gold chain dangled from his vest. He was dressed better than anyone there and the clothes looked new.

"Sybil Childs here is going to set an example for all the soiled doves and ladies of the night who think they can ply their trade in Angel's Camp," proclaimed Rader as he faced the crowd below him. "This town is decent. There's no place for prostitutes any more. It's a decent town now and the only way to run these harlots out is to send them down the road. One by one. Those what don't leave promply, I mean.

"Amen," mumbled the group of men who stood behind him on the porch. The porch was five feet higher than the street.

Sybil Childs struggled harder, tried to free her arms from the grasp of the two men who held her captive. They tightened their grip around her slender arms, dug strong fingers into the soft flesh beneath the long sleeves of her pale blue frock.

"I know you men, especially you miners, are used to these painted hussies," Rader continued to bellow, "but let some other town have them."

"Amen," came the muttered response from the others on the porch when Rader paused.

"Are you with me?" Rader shouted to the crowd below him. He shot a fist up into the air to show his power.

A half-hearted cheer went up. Rader glared at the crowd. He would not be satisfied with such a response.

"Well, do you want a decent town or not?" He took a step forward, punched the air again.

The cheer that arose was somewhat more fervent.

"It's not Sybil Childs we want!" Rader stormed. "She's just an example! We want Lucy Tucker! She's the one that made this unfortunate young girl into the fallen woman she is! Look at her! It's Lucy Tucker's doing. She's the madam here. She's the one we want out of town—forever!"

The crowd murmured. A few men yelled agreement.

Rader, anger flushing his features crimson, turned to the girl, grabbed the top of her dress and savagely ripped downward. His face contorted in fanatical rage as her breasts broke free of restraint, bobbed on her chest like honeydew melons.

Sybil kicked her foot, stabbed into Rader's shin with the hard toe of her button-top shoe.

Rader winced, jumped back. "You filthy little whore," he muttered, then turned again to the spectators. "Did you people see that? She's like a wild animal. Not fit to be a member of our society. I say to you, decent people, is this the kind of wench you want on the streets of Angel's Camp? The kind who will lift her skirts for any man with loose change in his pockets? The kind who will lure decent, moral men into her wicked web of lust and sin?"

"No," called a few of the men in the crowd.

Rader wanted more from them. He wanted to jar their sensibilities with his accusing words. He wanted the crowd riled up, like he was. He wanted them angry about the immorality that existed in their town. He wanted them raging mad, spitting fire.

"It's bad enough that Miss Lucy keeps such wicked women at her house of ill repute," Rader shouted, his face livid with rage, "but now the harlots are allowed to walk our streets. We caught Sybil Childs here in the

Dry Creek Saloon. The very saloon which some of you fine gentlemen patronize."

A rumble of discontent rippled through the crowd.

"Let me ask you innocent ladies out there. Do you want women like Sybil Childs or any of those other shameless harlots at Miss Lucy's to be on the streets of this respectable town? Do you want them out there enticing your very own husbands into their sinful beds? Do you want your husbands dirtied by these fallen women? Do you want your husbands bringing the disease home to you?" His voice rose to a fervent pitch.

"No! No!" cried the prim women of the town.

Bolt noticed a couple of the women latch on to their husbands, hold them tightly by the arm, as if to do so would keep them out of the bordello and the disease that was nurtured there. A couple of the men shifted uncomfortably, lowered their heads.

"Are we going to allow this to happen?" shouted Rader.

"No!" the women responded in unison.

"No, we're not," said Rader, shaking his fist for emphasis. Frantically seized with a righteous fervor that had him slavering at the mouth, he ripped Sybil's dress clear down the front, away from her body so that only her sleeves remained in place. Talbot removed the ragged sleeves from her arms, tossed them to the crowd below. Rader tore her long petticoat off, clutched at her panties and ripped them off.

The crowd gasped as Sybil stood stark naked in front of them. Some of them covered their faces with their hands or lowered their heads so the brims of their hats shielded their eyes from the sinful sight.

Talbot and Booker released their hold on the girl as

Rader grabbed her by the arm, pulled her down the steps toward the boiling kettle, the washtub full of musty feathers.

Bolt's jaw tightened with anger, disgust, as he watched the public display. He slid down off his horse, grabbed a blanket from his saddle. He rushed over to the naked girl.

Rader's eyes widened in surprise as he saw Bolt approaching. He let go of the girl's arm, started to protect himself, but Bolt didn't give him a chance.

Bolt shoved the man in the pin-striped suit back, out of the way, into the arms of the equally startled Dave Talbot who had followed Rader down the steps. Bolt draped the blanket around the frightened girl, pulled her close to him.

"This the way you uprighteous people allow a woman to be man-handled in your town?" Bolt shouted at the crowd. "Only savages would treat a human being this way. You call this man your leader? You're no better than he is."

Bolt saw Rader recover his balance, saw the sudden movement beyond Rader. He saw the small pocket pistol appear suddenly in Talbot's hand.

Bolt's hand streaked to his holster, fast as a striking snake. His pistol cleared leather, was cocked before Talbot could take aim.

Bolt shot from the waist. His aim, by instinct, was right on target.

Talbot screamed as the bullet slammed into his hand. His fingers contorted into grotesque appendages as the pocket pistol fell from his grip.

Calvin Rader started to go for his hide-out pistol.

Bolt swung on him, aimed his pistol at Rader's chest.

He waited, his eyes cold and glaring.

Rader pulled his hand away from his waistline.

"I'm not going to waste good bullets on the likes of you," Rader said in a loud voice. "I won't allow a gun-fight and risk having one of our decent citizens hit by a stray bullet. But you'd better listen up. This is an orderly meeting of the Merchants Association and you got no business here, stranger. You and your friend there better get out of town the same way you got here. Otherwise, you'll be leaving here like the other intruders. Toes down. Dragging the ground."

"If you represent the type of people who live here, I don't want any part of it. But this girl isn't going to suffer any more at your hands." Bolt slid his pistol back in the holster, turned and started to walk away with the blanket-clad girl.

"You're not taking her anywhere! She has to pay for her sins." Rader lunged at Bolt, knocked him sideways, away from Sybil.

The impact jarred Bolt's hat from his head, sent it flying to the dusty ground.

Sybil clutched the blanket around her neck, ducked to the side as Bolt swung around and jabbed Rader with a hard fist to the cheek. Sybil scooped Bolt's hat up from the ground, moved away from the fighting men.

Rader barely flinched. He plowed into Bolt's gut with both hands, his hard knuckles kneading the flesh like dough.

Bolt bent forward, brought his fist straight up, slammed it into Rader's jaw.

Rader's head snapped back. He shuffled sideways, staggered by the blow.

Bolt followed his advantage. He moved in close to the big man, brought his knee up, drove it up into Rader's crotch.

Rader moaned, clutched at his balls to stop the pain that drove through his loins.

As if by signal, three of Rader's friends leaped down from the porch, dashed to his aid. They were on Bolt like a swarm of wet bees, striking him from all sides. Two of them grabbed Bolt's arms, pulled him back against the porch rail. They held him there while the third one, a man named Hyker, pounded hard fists into Bolt's face. Bolt tautened his stomach muscles as they drove fists into his gut.

Tom Penrod jumped down from his horse the minute he saw the fight was no longer one-on-one. He rushed into the fray, threw his arm around Hyker's throat and pulled him away from Bolt. He moved around to the side, punched one of the men who was holding his friend. He slammed another blow into the man's head until he released Bolt.

With one arm free, Bolt whirled around, attacked the man who was clutching his other arm, knocked him away.

Fists flew as the spectators began to push and shove among themselves. A mob fight erupted as the townsmen and the rugged miners exchanged blows. Most of them didn't know who the enemy was. Didn't care.

The women scurried to the edge of the fighting arena, hiking their long dresses to keep them from dragging in the dirt. Several of the frightened women screamed hysterically while others covered their face with their hands, peering through their fingers to watch

13

the fight.

Bolt held his own, fighting off the attackers as they came. He punched men in business suits, traded blows with roughians, dodged the jabs of some when he could, took on two at a time when he had to.

Calvin Rader threaded his way through the melee, singled Bolt out. He planted a hard blow on Bolt's jaw before Bolt knew he was there.

Bolt's head snapped to the side under the impact. He turned back quickly, saw that Rader was prepared to deliver another staggering blow.

Knowing exactly how far he was away from the kettle of boiling tar, Bolt threw up both fists in front of his chest, danced away from Rader. Rader followed him, tried to land a punch. Bolt dodged the big fists, taunted the man, stepped back, moved sideways until he had Rader right where he wanted him.

Rader swung again. Missed.

Bolt brought his fist up hard, caught Rader on the chin.

The blow sent Rader staggering backwards, toward the boiling tar. Just in time, Rader saw the kettle behind him. His arms flew straight out from his body, moved in frantic circles as he fought to keep his balance.

Bolt reached out, gave a gentle push to Rader's shoulders. It was enough to send Rader sprawling backwards into the kettle of hot tar. Rader's new Stetson sailed off his head, landed in the kettle of black mush beside him.

When he hit the hot tar, Rader's scream pierced the air, echoed out above the scuffling noises of the fighting men. Some stopped fighting, looked in his direction. The liquid tar covered his backside, seared through his pin-striped suit, burned into his flesh. His legs dangled over the edge of the kettle, untouched by the hot tar. He struggled to get away from the heat but couldn't find the right leverage. Finally, in desperation, he plunged one arm down into the burning mass, managed to roll himself over, then pushed himself back out of the kettle. Black tar dripped from his suit, front and back. The heat from the tar penetrated the cloth, made Rader feel like a human torch.

Bolt pushed Rader into the washtub full of chicken feathers. The fighting among the other men came to a halt as they crowded around, stretched their necks to get a glimpse of Rader.

Some of the miners cheered when Calvin Rader crawled out of the tub. With feathers clinging to the hot tar, he looked like some mysterious, oversized bird. Ignoring the laughter that rippled through the crowd, Rader tore at his clothes, tried to free himself from the cloth oven that scalded his flesh. He stripped out of his clothes, dropped them to the ground.

Another cheer went up from the miners when Rader stood before them, naked except for the feather-covered hand that he used to try to cover his exposed genitals.

Bolt reached down, retrieved the Stetson from the kettle of tar, shoved the dripping hat on Rader's head.

"You'll regret this the rest of your short life," Rader hissed as Bolt turned and walked away.

"The show's over," Bolt announced. "Go on back home."

As the crowd started to disperse, Bolt went up to the porch, picked up Sybil's torn clothes and handed them to Tom.

"What do I do with these?" Tom asked.

"Just get our horses and follow me."

"Where're you going?"

"To take Sybil back to the bordello."

Leading Bolt's horse, Tom rode behind the couple as Bolt escorted the blanket-clad girl down the street.

Some of the miners fell in behind them, proclaiming Bolt their new hero.

"Thanks," Sybil said as she looked up at Bolt with sad blue eyes. "I don't even know your name."

"It's Bolt. I just don't cotton to seeing a lady being treated like that."

"I never been called a lady before," she giggled. "I appreciate what you did for me, but you'd better take heed of what Calvin Rader said."

"What's that?"

"You'd better get out of town while you still got your skin. Rader runs this town. He's got enough men on his side to give him all the power he wants. He won't stop until he runs all of us prostitutes out of town. If you stick around here, likely you won't live long enough to see the sun set."

Bolt kept walking, holding the girl close, but a cold shiver went up his spine. He knew she spoke the truth.

Chapter Two

The bordello sat at the edge of town, out of the way, inconspicuous. It looked like an ordinary two-story house. The sign that hung on the porch, above the steps, tagged it as MISS LUCY'S PLACE. But even the sign was vague. It might just as easily have referred to a boardinghouse or a home where the lady of the house took in sewing.

As Bolt approached the bordello with the shivering Sybil beside him, he noticed that a curtain in a front window was pulled aside as if someone were looking out. It didn't surprise him because the miners were making one helluva racket with their singing and cheering.

The curtain closed quickly when the noisy group reached the front of the building.

Tom tied the two horses to a hitchrail out front, grabbed Sybil's torn clothes from the saddle and followed Bolt and Sybil up the steps. The five miners clunked up the steps behind them, the porch creaking under the weight of their heavy boots.

Bolt tried the door, found it locked.

"Does Miss Lucy always keep her door locked?" Bolt asked.

"No, it's always open," Sybil said, "except for late at night when the bordello's closed."

Bolt tapped on the door, waited.

A minute later, the doorknob turned slowly. The door opened a crack.

Bolt pushed the door all the way open, found himself staring into the dark muzzle of a 12 gauge shotgun. He heard the ominous click as the hammer cocked. Behind the shotgun stood a tall, full-figured blonde with large breasts jutting over the top of her tight red satin dress. The woman's face was etched with hard features, a dark mole on one cheek. She glared at Bolt with accusing brown eyes.

"What have you done to Sybil?" she said.

Bolt removed his hat, opened his mouth to speak.

Sybil stepped in front of him, the blanket still clutched around her body.

"It's all right, Lucy. They're friends of mine. This is Mister Bolt and his friend, Mister Penrod. They just saved my life. You know the other men. They've all been here before."

Lucy Tucker glanced at the torn frock in Tom's hands then gave Bolt a long hard look. Finally, she lowered the shotgun and let the men inside.

The scent of perfume was overpowering when they stepped inside the long living room. Bolt glanced around, saw a small bar at one end, comfortable couches at the other. Like other whorehouses, the furnishings were bright and gaudy.

The miners sauntered over to the bar, began mixing

18

drinks for themselves, as was the custom at Miss Lucy's. Tom dropped Sybil's ragged clothes on a nearby table, joined Bolt and Sybil in the middle of the room. Lucy leaned the gun against the wall, turned to face the trio, waited for an explanation.

The frightened glitter gals surrounded them, all asking questions at once.

"I just went to the apothecary to buy something," Sybil said. "When I saw some members of the Merchants Association coming for me, I fled to the Dry Creek Saloon. They followed me in there and carried me outside. Calvin Rader said I had no business in the saloon and that he was going to make an example out of me. He set his men to work building a fire and gathering the feathers. Sent another one through the town to gather the people."

"I knew they were trying to put us out of business, but I didn't think they'd go this far," Lucy said. "A customer who came in a while ago said the Association was holding a meeting and that they were fixing to tar and feather somebody, but he didn't know who. I had no idea it was you, Sybil."

"I was so scared, I'm still shaking. Rader was just about to tar and feather me. He tore my clothes off in front of everyone and I wanted to die with embarrassment. Then the bully pulled me over to that kettle of hot tar which stank to high heaven. I don't think I'll ever get that smell out of my system. I came so close to getting dumped into that tar that my knees go weak when I think about it." Sybil shivered, then glanced up at Bolt and smiled. "Bolt rescued me just in time. You should have seen the way he stood up to Calvin Rader."

Lucy looked directly at Bolt, the hard lines in her

face softening.

"I don't know why you took it upon yourself to rescue Sybil," she said, "but we're all grateful. Thank you."

"I hear the gold mining boom has slowed down," said Bolt. "Think that's why the townspeople are trying to close your doors?"

Lucy glanced around the front room of her bordello, sighed.

"A mining town is a rough place to live, boom or no boom. If the diggings are good, it affects everyone here. It's not just the miners who get rich. The more gold they dump into the local coffers, the more all the businesses prosper, including ours. When times are good, people spend money like there was no tomorrow. But for us, business is just as brisk during hard times. Men tend to get depressed when the money stops flowing. That's when they need a good woman, some affection to lift their spirits. If they can't get it at home, they come here. And a lot of the men, especially the miners, don't have a woman. Some fellows leave their wives and children back East while they come out to California to strike it rich, figuring on sending for their families when they've made their fortune. It just isn't natural for a man to go without bedding a woman for any length of time. We provide a service to those who want it and I don't think that's any reason to give us a hard time. Sure, things are a little slow right now, but does that give Calvin the right to humiliate Sybil in a public demonstration?"

"It's you, he wants, Lucy," Sybil said, letting the blanket fall open to expose her bare breasts. "Rader said so. He said he wants to close the bordello, run you out of town. He thinks if he can get to each of us girls,

20

humiliate us in front of the townspeople, that you'll give up and leave."

"Rader's a hypocrite," Lucy snapped. "That man's got more lust in him than any of those miners. He's made obscene approaches to the girls in town, but only when no one was looking. I know, he approached me one day. The nerve of him wanting to close us down. He'd be the first one to visit the bordello if he dared, but he's afraid of his wife. Madge Rader rules him with an iron hand, that domineering bitch. She nags him from sunup to sunset. If she only knew that's the kind of behavior that drives men to whorehouses, she might be a little easier on him."

Something nudged at the back of Bolt's mind when he heard Rader's wife's name.

"I used to know a girl named Madge, but then I imagine there are a lot of girls with that name."

"Not many that I know of. Maybe it's the same girl."

"No. Come to think of it, the one I knew was far too smart to marry a man like Rader."

"Any girl in her right mind would be too smart to marry that galoot."

"From what I hear, Rader's the big gun in town," Bolt said.

"Not as far as I'm concerned," Lucy said indignantly. "A bunch of the storekeepers got together and formed the Merchants Association. They think just because they have an organization, they can tell everybody else what to do. They appointed Rader president of their group and he's let it go to his head. He's nothing more than a shopkeeper. Owns the mercantile store. Does that give him the right to boss everybody around?"

"I reckon not."

"Everybody was happy with the way things were until Rader started his campaign to clean up the town and close its last remaining bordello. I'm sure Madge Rader is behind that movement."

"I don't know about that, but Rader had a lot of support out there."

"You just don't understand how this town works, Mister Bolt. You're a stranger to these parts, aren't you?"

"Yep. We rode in a spell ago, just in time to see the town gathering for the tar and feathering."

"Well, if you're smart, you'll keep right on riding."

"That's the same thing Rader told me."

"What's your business here in Angel's Camp?" Lucy asked, her dark brown eyes studying Bolt's face.

"Why I came here to go into competition with you," Bolt smiled.

"Oh, no," gasped one of the glitter gals. The other girls looked at each other, shook their heads.

"It wouldn't work, mister," said a tall brunette named Tess. "There's no way the people in Angel's Camp would tolerate another bordello."

A murmur of agreement spread among the girls.

"She's right," said Lucy, blowing a strand of blond hair from her eyes. "If it weren't for the miners, we'd be out of business now. Funny, though, some of the very men who are trying to put us out of business used to be our best customers."

"I might be interested in a partnership," Bolt said. "How about joining forces?"

"What would you know about running a whorehouse?" snapped Lucy, the contempt she felt for men

22

showing in her sarcasm.

"Enough, considering I own a string of whorehouses across the West."

The other girls giggled, moved in closer to Bolt.

Lucy thought about his proposition for a moment.

"No. A partnership is out of the question," she said. "I'm ready to quit the business. There must be an easier way to make a living without having to kowtow to the whims of men like Calvin Rader."

"Then let me buy your place from you. I'll pay you a fair price."

"It's tempting, but I couldn't sell out to you and still have a clear conscience. The townspeople are likely to burn this place down at any moment. Then you'd have nothing to show for your money."

"If you'll stay here and fight these people, Tom and I will help you, won't we, Tom?" Bolt glanced over at his friend and saw that one of the glitter gals had draped herself around Tom's arm.

"Yair, sure," he replied without taking his eyes off the girl beside him.

"I can't see why you would want to help us since you hardly know us," said Lucy, "but I gladly accept your offer."

"There are conditions," said Bolt.

"Oh? You wouldn't be looking for a free piece of ass, would you?" The tone of her voice was suddenly suspicious, cutting with its sarcasm.

"No, ma'am. I reckon I get all the free ass I can handle without your help. You don't like men much, do you?"

"Not much."

"It shows."

23

"What are your conditions, Mister Bolt?"

"Number one is that you drop the 'mister.' Makes me sound like an old man."

"What else?"

"The girls must be treated decent . . ."

"I treat my girls decently," Lucy snapped. "Just as well as any other whores are treated."

"I imagine you do, but that's my point. They must be treated as well as a refined lady would be treated. They must be paid a decent salary. And rather than living in the shadows as they do, cut off from normal society, they must become active members of that society. They should go to quilting bees, go to church, attend box socials. Even become active in city government if they want to."

"We have never considered such a thing," Lucy said. "We know our place and that's where we stay."

"About time you considered it then. These girls are human beings and they have just as much right to enjoy a normal life as a schoolmarm or a seamstress. They should be allowed to participate in the activities that interest them."

"Yes, yes!" cried the girls in unison.

Bolt turned and smiled at the glitter gals.

"Instead of hiding, you girls should display your wares. Go out and mix with the people, turn on the charm."

The tall brunette named Tess, sidled up to Bolt, batted her eyelashes at him. When he looked at her, he couldn't help notice her creamy breasts that spilled over the top of her brief garment.

"Your ideas are radical," said Lucy. "They might work in a big town like San Francisco, but not here in

24

Angel's Camp. We're too far away from big-city life. You're talking about the girls mingling with society, but the townspeople won't even allow the bordello to exist because they think it tarnishes the image of the city. No way are they going to allow these harlots to be seen on the streets. Look what happened to Sybil just because she went to the apothecary."

"As long as you think of them as harlots or whores, that's the way they're going to be treated by the townspeople. Show these girls the respect they deserve and others will come to respect them, too. Let the girls mingle with ordinary people instead of keeping them locked up in a pen."

"Pens are for pigs," Lucy retorted, sticking her nose in the air indignantly. "I run a respectable place here."

"You're not very convincing, Lucy," Bolt said, leveling his eyes on hers. "I don't even think you believe what you're saying. I think somewhere along the line, you've formed the opinion that all men are cruel, untrustworthy beasts and that all women deserve to be treated like whores. I think someone hurt you and that you're punishing all men in general to make up for it."

Lucy reeled as if slapped in the face. She fought back the anger that boiled up inside her, the urge to strike back. She took a deep breath to calm herself, then faced Bolt again.

"You're quite blunt, aren't you?"

"I say it the way I see it, if that's what you mean."

"Maybe I've been wrong about keeping the girls here, but I don't want to risk having any more of them hurt or humiliated. After all, now we're talking about all of the merchants trying to force us out of business. As you say, Rader has a lot of power behind him. I don't trust Rader. I think he could be a very violent man if given the chance. I don't want to put your life in danger just to help us."

"But you don't know how brave Bolt is," Sybil spoke up. "He's also very fast with the gun. Bolt shot a pistol out of Dave Talbot's hand and you know how fast Dave is. Not only that, Bolt shoved Calvin Rader himself into the tar kettle, then pushed him into the tub of feathers. You should have seen it."

"Oh, no, you didn't," laughed Lucy. "I wish I could have seen it."

"Rader looked like a big bird," Sybil said. "That is until he stripped out of his clothes when the heat from the tar began to sizzle his skin."

"You mean he took off all his clothes in front of everybody?" Lucy doubled over in laughter, the first time she had laughed in a long, long time.

The glitter girls joined in the laughter, cheered for justice accomplished.

"It's true," said a miner who ambled over to them, a drink in hand. "I seed it with my own eyes. Don't worry about Rader. His pecker ain't big enough to interest any of your gals. He don't even have hair on his chest."

The girls giggled among themselves.

"Well, Bolt," said Lucy, "it looks like you're just the man we need on our side. Are you sure you want to help us?"

"I wouldn't have offered if I didn't mean it."

"Rader and his bunch can be pretty tough."

"I reckon I've been up against tougher."

"Would you care to stay here at the bordello?" Lucy asked. "I have a small bedroom upstairs that is vacant."

"Might be a good idea in case Rader pulls any more

26

of his shenanigans."

"You and Tom will have to bunk together, but I think you can manage."

Tom stepped forward, took his hat off.

"If it's all the same to you, ma'am, I reckon I'll stay at the hotel in town," Tom said. "You don't know what it's like sleeping with my friend here. Bolt snores like an elephant with a summer cold."

"Fine with me," Bolt said. "At least I won't have to smell those rank socks of yours."

"It's settled then," Lucy said, ignoring their good-natured kidding. "Let's have a drink on it and then I'll take you up and show you your room. Sybil, you'd better go up and get some clothes on before you catch your death of cold."

Sybil turned and left the group, secretly pleased that Bolt would be staying with them. She walked up the steps to the second floor of the large house. The private bedrooms of the girls who worked there were on one side of the hall. Opposite them, along the other side of the long hall, were the smaller rooms where the customers were entertained for a fee.

As she passed the vacant room that she knew would be Bolt's, she smiled to herself. Her own bedroom was right next door. She felt safer already just knowing Bolt would be so close.

She felt something else, too. She felt the hot surge of desire flow into loins as she wondered what it would be like to be bedded by a man who was as handsome and rugged as Bolt.

If she worked it right, she could have Bolt to herself when she wasn't working. It would be easy to slip into his room at night. There were no locks on the doors.

27

Chapter Three

The five miners, dressed in dusty, faded overalls, stepped aside to make room for Bolt and Tom to join them at the bar in Lucy's neat but modest bordello. The bar stool scraped against the hardwood floor as Bolt pulled it back away from the counter. He slid onto the seat as Tom settled onto a high stool next to him.

Lucy stepped around behind the bar, reached up on a high shelf and brought down an unopened bottle of Downings whiskey. She wiped the dust from the bottle with a clean towel, then picked up two clean glasses and placed them on the counter in front of Bolt and Tom.

Bolt set his hat down on the counter, flexed his trail-stiff shoulder muscles. A moment later, he felt the slight pressure on his shoulders as someone touched him there. The hackles on the back of his neck rose instantly as if a gun had been placed against the back of his head. He quickly stifled the instinct to go for his gun.

"You need a massage," husked the tall brunette behind him. Tess dug her long fingers into his shoulders, then rubbed the flesh with the palms of her

28

hands. She ran one hand under his arm, around to his chest. She leaned into him, pressed her breasts against his back as she let her hand fall into his lap.

Lucy did not miss the bold movement on Tess' part. Normally, it wouldn't have bothered her. After all, she paid Tess and the other girls to fondle the men who came there, to entice the customers to their beds. But Bolt was not a customer.

Lucy's eyes flashed with resentment as a twinge of jealousy stabbed at her heart. She considered Bolt her own guest, not up for grabs by the harlots who worked for her, but she realized that she had no hold on him. He had offered to help her, but other than that, he was just a stranger in town. She didn't even know him well enough to call him a friend. She shook the brief twinge of jealousy off, surprised by her own feelings. She hadn't admitted to herself that she found Bolt attractive, fascinating. She hadn't allowed herself to think of any man in those terms in a long time.

"All Bolt needs now, Tess, is a drink," she said, trying to keep the sarcasm from her voice.

Tess looked up, saw the look of warning in Lucy's eyes. Her lower lip pooched out in a pout, Tess slid her hand up to Bolt's shoulder, gave one final squeeze before she moved it away. She took one step to the side, squirmed into the small space between Bolt and Tom.

Feeling almost ashamed that she had chastised Tess, Lucy poured the two tumblers half full of her good whiskey, pushed them toward Bolt and Tom.

"Aren't you going to join us?" Bolt asked as he held his glass up.

"I don't normally drink during working hours," she said, "but I guess this is a special occasion." She

29

reached for another glass, poured two fingers in it, then offered the whiskey to the others.

The five miners and the other glitter gals crowded around to get their share of the drinks. Then they all gathered around Bolt and Tom, anxious to rub elbows with the celebrated pair.

Lucy sipped the whiskey, peered over the top of her glass at Bolt. For a brief moment, their eyes locked and Bolt felt the magnetism between them. There was a challenge in her eyes, but behind that challenge, Bolt saw the pain and sadness, the veil of mystery that surrounded her. He wondered who had hurt her. He studied her face, saw that she was not as old as he had first thought. He guessed her to be in her late twenties. He liked the dark mole on her face. More than a beauty mark, it added to her air of mystique.

The old miner who had spoken up before, sidled up next to Bolt. He slapped Bolt on the back, smiled with half of his front teeth missing.

"Mighty proud to know ya, boys," he shouted in Bolt's ear. "The name's Hard Luck Hal. These here are my friends. Chester, Wiley, Clem and Eli Dingledorf, better known as Dinger. You boys is doing us a great service and if we can be of help, just give us a holler."

"Will do," Bolt said, turning his attention to the miners.

"Yep, you're sure enough a hero," said Dinger, a tall emaciated man with face like leather from being out in the sun too long. "But I'd be watchin' over my shoulder were I you. Calvin Rader ain't likely to let you get away with making a fool out of him."

"I'll be careful," Bolt smiled. As he drank his drink, the miners gawked at him, questioned him about his pistol, his shooting ability and a dozen other things.

Tom, more interested in Tess than the fame and glory of the moment, stood up, slid his arm around Tess' waist and led her to a couch at the other end of the room.

"If you're ready, I'll take you up and show you your room," Lucy said to Bolt as the miners turned their attention to the glitter gals.

"I'm ready," Bolt smiled, glad for the excuse to get away from the noisy celebration. He finished his drink, pushed the glass aside. As Lucy came from behind the bar, he stood up, followed her toward the staircase with its polished banister. As he walked up the stairs behind her, he couldn't help but notice the way Lucy's tight red gown clung to her flared buttocks, the way her hips shifted with each step she climbed. It was like watching two kids fighting under a blanket.

When they reached the top of the stairs, he saw Sybil who was just coming out of her room. She had dressed in a gaudy red costume that was brief enough to show her slim stockinged legs. The skin-tight outfit cinched her waistline in so it was very tiny and pushed her creamy white breasts up over the top of the shiny material. She had brushed out her long blond hair and applied the heavy makeup of her trade so that she looked more like a delicate China doll than the girl he had first seen in town when she wore a proper street dress and less paint on her face.

As Lucy stopped in front of the room that was to be Bolt's, Sybil smiled at Bolt, batted her eyelashes.

"Would you like me to show Bolt his room?" she said to Lucy without taking her eyes off Bolt.

"No, I'll do it myself," Lucy snapped.

31

There it was again, Bolt thought. The sarcasm, the rudeness. It was as if Lucy was protecting him from the girls. Or was she jealous? he thought.

"I just thought if you were busy . . ." Sybil said in a husky voice.

"I'm not that busy," Lucy retorted. "You're needed downstairs to take care of the customers. The miners are ready to spend their money."

"But I'd rather . . ."

"Sybil . . ." Lucy warned.

"All right, I'm going," Sybil pouted. She patted her chest. "Oh, I forgot my necklace. I'll go get it and then go downstairs."

As Lucy opened the door to Bolt's room, Sybil disappeared into her own room next door. Sybil walked across the room, picked her necklace up from the dresser, was headed for the door when she heard the voices from the next room. She stepped closer to the thin wall between the two rooms and listened.

"Don't be fooled by Sybil's boldness," Lucy said in the next room. "The girls are taught to come on strong to all the men. I'll have a word with her and make it plain that you're a guest here, not a customer."

Sybil wanted to run next door and tell Lucy to mind her own damned business. But she was willing to bide her time. She knew she would have the opportunity to be alone with Bolt later. After all, Lucy slept downstairs at night, in the living quarters at the back of the house. Lucy would never have to know what went on upstairs.

"Don't worry about that," Bolt said. "I make it a policy never to sleep with whores."

"Oh? You too good for them?" Lucy said smugly.

"No, not at all. I consider them ladies, but I never mess with the girls. A long-standing rule of mine."

"That go for the madams, too?" Lucy asked.

"Why? Are you offering?"

"No. Just curious."

In her own room, Sybil was stunned by Bolt's words. Who did he think he was to be so selective? She still wanted him, but there was a new challenge to it now. She'd show both of them she was just as good as they were. She slipped out of her room, went downstairs to join the miners, determined to prove Bolt wrong.

Bolt glanced around at the small room, saw that there was only a single bed and a dresser with a porcelain water bowl and pitcher setting on it, a small nightstand next to the bed and an oval-shaped braided rug on the hardwood floor.

"I'm sorry it isn't bigger," Lucy said.

"It'll do."

As they started to leave the room, Bolt noticed the door handle.

"No lock on the door?" he asked.

"Not necessary," Lucy said. "We're family here and we respect each other's privacy. We lock the front and back doors after hours. Why? Do you think Rader and his men would come here looking for you?"

"Wouldn't surprise me at all."

Calvin Rader sat at a table in the back room of the Dry Creek Saloon, hidden from the curious stares of the other customers. Dave Talbot, the only other person in the small room, paced the floor, his mangled shooting hand wrapped in a handkerchief.

Rader felt ridiculous in his tar and feather-covered suit that made him look twice as bulky as he was, but he had put the suit back on just as soon as it had cooled enough. It was the only thing he had to wear until he could get home and change clothes.

The suit was ruined, he was sure. It was beyond cleaning or saving. That didn't bother him nearly as much as the fact that he had been humiliated in front of his peers. He was the laughing stock of Angel's Camp. Even some of his own men had laughed when he had pulled himself out of the kettle of hot tar and then been promptly dumped into the tub of feathers. That was bad enough, but the ultimate embarrassment had come when he tore his burning clothes away from his body and the crowd had cheered. It made him feel like some damn side show in the circus.

"I'm gonna kill that fuckin' bastard," Rader raged as he plucked the stubborn feathers from the tar that covered his left hand.

"Not if I kill him first," Talbot seethed, stopping in front of Rader just long enough to take a healthy swig from his glass of whiskey.

"Wonder who he is. I never saw him before." Rader winced when he tried to peel some of the tar from his wrist.

"He goes by the name of Bolt. His partner's name is Tom Penrose or Penrod, somethin' like that."

"How do you know?" Rader's eyebrows shot up as he eyed Talbot suspiciously.

"Pete Booker told me. Pete overheard the strangers introducing themselves to that painted whore. Outlaws, I'd say. Both of 'em. The one what shot me is a mean-looking sonofabitch."

"And mighty damned fast with a gun, from what I saw. Well, he's barkin' up the wrong tree if he thinks he can come in here and butt into our business. Look what he did to my clothes. Ruined them for good. And my hand. It'll take forever to get this damned tar off." Rader gulped whiskey from his glass, poured another drink from the bottle they had ordered, then went back to the tedious job of plucking feathers from the hardened tar on his hand.

"What're you bitchin' about?" Talbot snorted. "All you lost was your dignity. Look at me. My bloody hand's shot to shit and it hurts like hell. Likely, I'll never be able to use it again."

"Pretty fancy shooting, wasn't it," Rader said. He took another swallow of whiskey, glanced at Talbot's bandaged hand. "He shot that pistol out of your hand in the bat of an eye. And you're supposed to be a fast draw. That strike you as odd? That two strangers ride into town just as were about to tar and feather that hussy?"

"Say it straight, Rader."

"I think he's a hired gun., I think Lucy Tucker hired him when she found out we were gonna close her down."

"You're talkin' through your hat, Calvin. Lucy hain't had no time to hire her a gunny. The Merchant's Association didn't even vote on it until last night."

"Well, it don't matter. That bastard you call Bolt is here and he's siding with them harlots. Least ways, he was seen to take that tramp Sybil back over to the bordello. He smells like trouble to me and I don't want him around to mess up our plans. We gotta figure out a way to get rid of him. Permanently."

"I agree, but for different reasons. Nobody shoots me like he did and gets away with it. He's as good as dead. Only trouble is, my hand is no damned good now. It's gonna take me a month to learn to handle a gun with my other hand."

"We'll have to get the sheriff to arrest him. Lock him up."

"Luke Pettibone? He don't know his ass from a hole in the ground. I say we hire a gunny to do him in."

"Kinda risky if anyone found out we hired a gunman to kill a man. I mean, we're supposed to be cleaning up this town, getting rid of crime and undesirables."

"That's what we'd be doing by getting rid of Bolt and his friend. How about it. And I know just the man who can handle it. Hardy Bragg, a friend of mine from Sacramento. Fastest gun in the West. I could tell you stories about him that would curl your hair. I can send for him, have him up here day after tomorrow."

"No, Dave, we'd better let the law handle it. Keep our noses clean. Let's go pay a visit to Pettibone."

At the sheriff's office, Luke Pettibone leaned back in his chair and listened to the two men plead their case. He didn't like either of them, but he knew that Calvin Rader was the power in Angel's Camp and he wanted to stay on Rader's good side. Luke thought Rader was wrong for staging that tar and feathering ceremony and Luke had intentionally stayed away from the public display so he wouldn't have to cross Rader. Luke waited patiently until the two men were finished telling their story, and then he spoke.

"I know that the Merchant's Association is doing

everything it can to make this town more respectable," he said, "and I respect you for that. But I can't arrest a man without cause just because he's a stranger in town."

"Isn't shooting a man 'cause' enough?" said Dave Talbot, holding his bandaged hand up for the sheriff to see.

Pettibone leaned forward, puffed on his cigar.

"Not if it's in self defense," he said. "And from what I've heard, that's what it was. Self defense. You pulled your pistol first, didn't you, Talbot?"

"Yes, but . . ."

"Then you've got no case and neither do I."

"But he's an outlaw," Rader protested.

"You got any proof?" said the sheriff.

"No, but you're the one with access to the records and wanted posters. You do some checking and you'll see that we're right."

"I'll tell you what I'll do, gentlemen. I'll run a check on this Bolt character and if I find that he's a wanted man, as you say, I'll arrest him right away." Luke stood up, signalling that the conversation was over.

Rader started to say something else, but Pettibone cut him off.

"I'll do all I can, but you must remember that you are the ones who want an honest town. I do too, and that is why I won't risk arresting an innocent man."

Properly dismissed, Rader and Talbot left the sheriff's office, walked to their horses.

"Damned cautious asshole," Talbot grumbled. "I told you he was gutless."

"What was the name of that gunny you mentioned?" Rader said.

"Bragg. Hardy Bragg. You want me to send fo him?"

"Yes. Just make sure he never mentions my name And pay him well. This is one job I don't wan botched."

"Don't worry, Calvin. Bragg doesn't fail. He'll tak care of Bolt and be gone without anyone knowing h was here. This is Wednesday afternoon. I'll have hin up here by Friday afternoon. Bolt will be dead befor sunrise on Saturday."

Chapter Four

Madge Rader gasped when her husband entered the room.

"What happened to you?" she said.

"You're the one who wanted that bordello closed," he said defensively.

"But your clothes. They're ruined. Just look at you. You'll never get that tar off your suit."

"So, I've got other suits." Rader hated his wife for not caring about his scorched tar-covered hand. He should have known that she wouldn't offer to help him get the tar off his hand like other wives would if their husbands came home in a similar circumstance.

He loved Madge at one time, when they were first married two years before. He had thought her the most elegant woman he had ever seen, the most beautiful with her pretty dresses, the long red hair and those green eyes that had once held him under their hypnotic spell. She had started harping at him shortly after they were married and as her nagging increased, his love had faded. They merely tolerated each other now and she still allowed him to partake of his conjugal rights in their bed, but she made certain that she considered it her wifely duty and not a privilege.

There were times when he wanted to leave her, but he couldn't bring himself to make the move. He needed her and she knew it. It wasn't just her sophisticated beauty which caused him to be the envy of every man in town that kept him tied to her. He was sure that having a beautiful wife helped him to gain the power he had, but he needed her for another reason. Her money. She was independently wealthy when he met her, claiming she got her money from an inheritance. She had bought the mercantile store for him, the house they lived in, the furniture they sat on.

Without her, he would have nothing. That is why he tolerated her constant nagging, why he gave in to her every demand.

"How did you ever allow this to happen?" she taunted.

Calvin explained to her that he was trying to make an example out of the harlot so that Lucy Tucker would give up and close her despicable bordello.

"A stranger rode up and caught me unawares. No way I could defend myself," he said lamely. "The bastard dumped me into the kettle of tar and the feathers and that was it. I could have gotten Bolt but that tar was burning through my clothes and he got away."

At the mention of Bolt's name, Madge gasped. Her face drained of color.

"Did you say Bolt?" she asked.

"Yeah. He was the one what shoved me into that mess. He's responsible for my clothes being all messed up. And my hand. Me and Dave went to the sheriff about it and Pettibone is gonna arrest Bolt. Ought to make the bastard buy me a new suit."

"You sure the name was Bolt?" Madge asked.

"Yes, I'm sure," Rader said, annoyed with his wife's continuous questioning. He glanced at her, saw the startled look on her face. "Why? Do you know him?"

"No, uh," she stammered. "No. It's just an unusual name. I mean, I don't know anyone in town by that name."

"I told you it was a stranger who did this to me," Rader explained again. He felt like he was talking to a blank wall. Either she didn't care enough to listen to his story or she was just plain dumb. Maybe he'd never understand what went on in her head.

Madge covered her mouth with her fingers. Her green eyes which were usually sensual bedroom eyes, widened to large circles. Suddenly, she turned and fled from the room.

Rader shook his head. He wondered what the hell was the matter with his wife this time, but he was glad to avoid her nagging for even a few moments.

Madge was shaking by the time she reached her room upstairs. She went inside, closed the door behind her and sat down on the cushioned chair in front of her dressing table. She buried her head in her hands, fought back the tears that stung her eyes.

Her body trembled from the shock at hearing Bolt's name after all this time. As she raised her head, she wondered if it could be someone else with the same name. But even as she thought it, she knew better. There could only be one Bolt.

At first, she was angry. Angry that Bolt had come to

41

her town and caused trouble, interferred with the Merchants Association's efforts to close down the bordello. That would be like Bolt to do that. He always did stick up for the whores.

She picked the brush up from the dressing table, ran it through her hair. When she glanced in the mirror and saw her pale face, her anger turned to fear.

Bolt was in town and he was a threat to her security. She couldn't let him find out that she lived in Angel's Camp. She had to make sure that he never saw her. He could ruin her life forever. She thought of ways to get rid of him, to wipe him out of her life forever. She knew her husband wanted to have Bolt arrested. Now she would have to put pressure on Calvin to get rid of Bolt at any cost. She didn't care how Calvin did it. Just so Bolt wasn't around to interfere with her present life.

Dave Talbot drank whiskey that night at the Dry Creek Saloon to ease the pain in his broken hand. He drank so much, in fact, that he was feeling no pain at all when Tom Penrod came through the batwing doors, followed by the five miners who insisted on continuing their celebration.

After spending a passionate hour with Tess, and paying for her services, Tom had ridden back to the middle of town, checked into the Angels Hotel. Bolt and the miners had joined him for supper at a small cafe and after Bolt left to return to the bordello, Hard Luck Hal had persuaded Tom to join them for a drink at the saloon.

Hunched over the bottle on the table in front of him, Talbot watched Penrod and his followers make their way to the long bar. With blurry eyes, he tried to focus on Penrod's features. His head bobbed drunkenly as he tried to find Bolt in the group of men. He wanted Bolt. He wanted to blow his hand away, show him what it felt like. Hatred seeped through his fogged brain and he could think of nothing else. He couldn't find Bolt in the sea of blurred faces.

It didn't matter. He'd shoot Bolt's friend. That would be the same thing.

Talbot reached for the nearly empty bottle in front of him. It took him two tries before he could pick it up with his left hand. He poured the contents into his glass, sloshing most of it on the table. He tipped his head back, poured the whiskey down his throat, slammed the glass down on the table. He fumbled for his pistol, finally brought it out of its holster. He set it on the table, in the puddle of spilled whiskey. His mind blanked out, he stared at the pistol for a long minute before he could remember what to do with it. Using one hand, he finally managed to pull the hammer back.

Holding the pistol in his left hand, he stood up, promptly lurched to the left, bounced against the wall. He held the weapon straight down, against his pantleg, and started for the bar. Listing to one side, he staggered around the tables, bumped into empty chairs, took up position a few feet behind Tom. He wavered there for a moment while he brought the pistol up, tried to steady his hand as he aimed it at Tom's head.

He lurched forward.

The cocked pistol jammed into Tom's back.

Stunned by the sudden pain that jolted through him, Tom gasped.

"I gonna kill you sombitch," Talbot slurred.

43

Tom stiffened, froze in place, not daring to turn around with the hard pistol jammed against his back.

"Kill you 'n' Bolt," Talbot mumbled, his words slurred together. He tried to pull the trigger, but he had neither coordination nor strength in his finger muscles.

Dinger, the miner standing next to Tom, turned, realized what was happening. He took one quick step toward Talbot, shoved him with his shoulder.

Talbot staggered sideways. Before he could regain his balance, Dinger brought his arm up, knocked the pistol from the drunken man's hand.

Hard Luck Hal and Chester turned in time to grab Talbot as he started to fall. Hal brought Talbot back to a standing position and Chester slammed his fist into Talbot's nose. Blood spurted out of both nostrils, splattered on Talbot's shirt.

Tom whirled around, faced his attacker.

"You dirty sonofabitch!" he shouted. "So you thought you were going to shoot me in the back." Tom let go with both fists, one in Talbot's jaw, the other in the man's gut.

Talbot staggered back, fell to the floor.

Tom moved in, stood over him. He raised his foot, poised his boot above Talbot's good hand.

"I ought to break your other hand so you could never jack yourself off again," Tom threatened. He looked down and saw that Talbot was oblivious to any threats. He lowered his foot without striking the man, turned away disgusted.

"Do you want us to work him over?" asked Hard Luck Hal, a sinister grin on his face.

"Yeah," said Dinger, spoiling for a fight. "We'll make hash out of his face."

"No," Tom said. "Let the bastard go. He's a loser any way you look at it. Just throw him out on his ass. Maybe he'll learn not to pick a fight when he's full of booze."

Four of the miners lifted Talbot up, each holding on to one of his limbs. The drunk man mumbled a slurred protest as they carried him to the batwing doors. They swung his body back, started counting.

"One . . . two . . ." On "three" they gave him a mighty heave.

Talbot bounced once on the porch, crashed through the railing and landed on the hard ground four feet below.

"That'll teach ya," shouted Hard Luck Hal. "Don't bother us no more."

The others cheered, watched long enough to see him get up on his knees and one hand and crawl away into the darkness.

Tom bought the next round of drinks, offered a toast when the barkeep brought the drinks.

"For saving my life," he said as he held his glass high.

"Hell, he couldn't have killed ya," said Dinger modestly. "He were too drunk to shoot."

"You're right about one thing, Dinger," Tom smiled. "He was too drunk to shoot, but you're damned lucky that pistol didn't go off by accident when he shoved it in my back. Otherwise, you'd be buying your own drinks now."

"I'll drink to that," grinned Hard Luck Hal.

After speaking briefly to Lucy when he got back to the bordello, Bolt went right to his room. He knew that

45

Sybil and a couple of the other girls were busy across the hall with some of the miners who had come in after a day of working their claims. The three girls who were still downstairs had spoken, smiled their lovely smiles, but had not approached him.

He lit the coal oil lantern, replaced the sparkling glass chimney only to see it begin to cloud with dark smoke. He adjusted the wick, closed the door to his room. He didn't much like the idea of not having a lock on the door, but he guessed if the girls felt safe without a lock, he should too. He carried the lantern across the room, placed it on the nightstand. His saddlebags and bedroll were still on the bed where he had dumped them earlier. He had planned to empty the saddlebags, put his belongings in the dresser drawers, but now he was tired. He and Tom had been up before dawn, riding the rough trail all day in order to make Angel's Camp before dark. Persistence had paid off. They had reached Angel's Camp two hours ahead of schedule, but now, his muscles felt the strain.

He moved the saddlebags and bedroll off the bed, set them down in a corner of the room. He unbuckled his gunbelt, draped it around one of the brass bedposts at the head of the bed, hung his Stetson on the same post. He sat on the edge of the bed, removed his boots and socks, unbuttoned his shirt and peeled it off. He stood up, threw the covers back to expose clean white sheets, leaned over and blew the lantern out. He slipped out of his trousers, let them fall to the floor in a heap beside the bed. He stretched out on the bed, naked except for his undershorts, let the softness of the feather mattress soak into his tired muscles.

Despite his intention to sleep lightly with one ear

tuned to his door, he fell into a deep sleep minutes after he hit the bed.

Sometime in the middle of the night, Bolt awoke with a start.

He felt his mattress jiggle and knew someone was at his bedside.

His hand shot up to his gunbelt.

He felt the bed move again with the weight of the intruder.

Frantic, he fumbled in the dark for his pistol.

"Don't worry, Bolt. It's just me," whispered the voice.

It was a woman's voice, soft and husky.

Chapter Five

Bolt let his hand fall back down to his chest. He squinted his eyes, peered into the darkness, tried to make out the face of the intruder. The scent of delicate perfume filled his nostrils.

"Sybil?" he said.

"No. It's me. Lucy."

"Lucy! What the hell . . ."

In the next room, Sybil stirred in her bed, awakened by a bad dream.

Fear struck her heart when she heard the faint voices. For a moment, she thought her dream was a reality, that there was really someone in her room who was going to grab her and carry her to the kettle of dark, foul-smelling, bubbling tar.

Sybil heard the voices again, was relieved when she realized they were coming from the next room. As she brought herself fully awake, she remembered that Angie had moved out two days ago and that room now belonged to Bolt. Who could he be talking to at that hour of the night? Since her bed was against the thin wall that separated the two rooms, she scooted over closer to the wall, listened to see if Bolt was in some kind of danger.

"Were you expecting Sybil?" Lucy said.

"I wasn't expecting anybody. What time is it?"

"A little after three o'clock."

"What's the matter?"

"I'm scared, Bolt."

"Did something happen?"

"Not to me. One of our customers told me there was trouble at the Dry Creek Saloon earlier tonight. Your friend was involved."

"Tom? What happened?" Bolt propped himself up on his elbow, pulled the sheet up to his waist, covering his bare legs, his undershorts.

Pale moonlight filtered through the curtain on the window near his bed. As his eyes adjusted to the darkness, he could make out the outline of Lucy's head, her light-colored hair.

The old bed frame squeaked and groaned when Lucy sat down on the edge of the narrow bed. Her heady scent became stronger as she moved closer.

Bolt drank in her fragrance, felt the warmth of her presence.

"Dave Talbot tried to kill him . . ."

"Jeeez, why didn't you tell me earlier?"

"It turned out to be a minor skirmish. Tom didn't get hurt, but he could have been killed just as easily. Seems that Talbot got drunk and pulled a gun on him."

Bolt relaxed.

"Tom's a big boy. He can take care of himself."

"I'm sure he can. It's just that I thought if Rader got wind of the incident, he might come looking for you."

"Why? I wasn't even there."

"I know, but you and Tom are friends and Rader's not the type to forget a grudge. You probably think me silly, but I haven't been able to get to sleep. I keep hearing strange noises. Probably just my imagination, but I'm frightened."

"Fear can be a powerful thing, whether it's real or imagined." Bolt reached a hand out to comfort her. He felt the smooth fabric of her robe, the softness of her flesh beneath it. Just as he realized his hand was on her thigh, he felt her stiffen, shift positions to move away from his touch.

"Yes, it can," she said.

"You're afraid of more than strange noises, aren't you, Lucy?"

"What do you mean?" she said, clearing her throat self-consciously.

"You told me this afternoon that you didn't much like men, but you're afraid of them, afraid of me."

"I'm not afraid of you, Bolt. But yes, certain men scare the hell out of me."

"Are you scared of those men, or are you afraid of your own feelings toward them? There's a difference, you know."

"You've got a point. Depends on the man, I suppose. I am terrified by violent men. Like Rader and his men, or outlaws. I'm quite sure they're capable of physically abusing a woman under certain circumstances. Other men, well, I'm probably afraid of my own feelings more than anything else. I just don't allow myself to get involved with any of them. Saves a lot of heartache that way."

"Who hurt you, Lucy? Who has caused you so much pain that you're afraid to have a normal relation with a man?"

"My husband," she sighed as if it was a great weight off her shoulders just to admit it.

"Want to talk about it?"

"I never have. Not to anyone."

"Sometimes it helps. Was he a violent man?"

"Not at first and never very often. He was a kind and gentle man, a loving husband. I thought I was the luckiest girl alive when he asked me to marry him. He studied very hard to become a successful lawyer. We lived in Sacramento and when we became involved with the upper crust of society, he began to drink at parties and social gatherings. As the pressures of his practice increased, so did his drinking. It finally got to the point where he couldn't handle his liquor. We would come home from a party and he would call me names, shout at me. Then it got so bad that he began beating me when he was drunk."

"Did you leave him?"

Lucy wiped a tear from her eye, took a deep breath.

"No. I stuck with him till the end. I knew he wasn't himself when he was drinking. It was like a sickness with him. He never remembered beating me up the next morning and he was very ashamed. I thought I could help him, but I never could. Once he started drinking, he was a different man."

"I've known men like that."

"That last night, almost five years ago, we had been

51

to a party and Paul was drinking. After the party, he brought a lawyer friend home with us. Both men were drunk and continued to drink. I went on to bed. About an hour later, Paul came storming into the bedroom with his friend, John. Paul called me a whore because I wouldn't get up and find another bottle of whiskey when theirs was empty. I was afraid of him, afraid to get out of bed and get another bottle even though I knew where it was. Paul was furious and said he was going to prove I was a whore. He yelled at me, told me I had to have sex with John right then and there, in my very own bed, or he would beat me up. He said he wanted me to show him I was a whore. John was so drunk, he went along with Paul and I'm sure he didn't realize what he was doing. John was far too drunk to get into me, or to even get it hard, but he took his clothes off and tried. When Paul saw the two of us in bed together without any clothes on, it must have caused a shock to his system because he went all crazy. He pulled a gun and shot at the bed. Killed his best friend, although I will always think the bullet was meant for me. I got up and managed to get the gun away from Paul. He was babbling and staggering. I talked him into letting me help him into the living room and I calmed him down. When he passed out on the sofa, I rode to the sheriff's office for help. There was an investigation and a jury trial. Paul swore up and down that he didn't remember shooting his friend and I believed him. So did the judge, I think. Paul got a light sentence, five years in prison instead of death, because the judge declared that Paul wasn't in control of his senses when the crime was committed."

"Is Paul still in prison?"

"As far as I know, although his time should be up soon. I went to see him once in prison. He asked my forgiveness. I forgave him, but I knew I could never trust him again. After the trial, the word got around town that I was a loose woman because I slept with Paul's best friend, which wasn't really true. I left Sacramento shortly after that, in total disgrace. I came here to forget about it."

"And you've kept all men at arm's length ever since."

"Yes. If I couldn't trust my own husband, who could I trust?"

"I'm sorry," Bolt said. "About your husband."

"I guess I felt like a whore after that," she said after a moment. "When I came here, I bought this big house, figuring on turning it into a boardinghouse so I could make enough money to exist. I wasn't qualified to be a schoolmarm but I could cook and keep house. The first boarders were two young ladies. Pretty little things. Wholesome. I didn't know it at the time, but they were prostitutes. That is, they were entertaining men in their rooms for pay. When I discovered what was going on, I overlooked it, as long as there was no trouble. After all, who was I to criticize their lifestyle?"

Bolt didn't respond to her question. She didn't expect him to. He knew she had to tell her story, get it off her chest.

"Gradually, this place got to be known as the local bordello," she said. "Other girls came here, begging to work as prostitutes. The men were always well-behaved and I saw the need for a bordello in this small town where there are so many men without women. Besides, my past didn't seem important to anyone. Nobody asked questions. So I went into the business.

53

That's why these rooms are so small. There were fou[r]
large bedrooms upstairs, two on each side of the hall.
had them partitioned off so each bedroom becam[e]
three smaller rooms. There's never been any troubl[e]
here until now. Until Rader and the other merchant[s]
decided that the bordello was a disgrace to the community. I'm ready to give it all up. Move to anothe[r]
town."

"You can't keep running away from life, Lucy." Bo[lt]
sat up. In the faint light from the window, he could se[e]
the tears running down Lucy's cheeks.

"But I don't . . ."

"You ran away from Sacramento when the going go[t]
rough. And now you're ready to buckle under t[o]
Rader's whims. If you believe what you're doing i[s]
right, you've got to stay and fight for it. It won't be eas[y]
but you'll feel better about yourself."

"That's easy for you to say. You're a man. You aren'[t]
afraid of anything."

"There have been times when I've been scared as hel[l]
but I don't run away."

"I'm glad you're here, Bolt. I just feel guilty abou[t]
asking you to help me when it's my battle."

"You didn't ask. I offered. Besides it's all right to as[k]
for help when you need it. I do. Tom may seem like [a]
carefree chap who goes through life with no worrie[s]
but when I need him, he's right there. He's a good ma[n]
to have as a friend."

"So are you, Bolt. I consider you my friend. I gues[s]
that's why I told you everything. I couldn't handle a[ll]
the guilt and fear by myself anymore. Paul used to b[e]
the best friend I had. I could talk to him about anythin[g]
and he always made me feel better. Sometimes I wish

could wake up and find that everything was just a bad dream and that things were the way they used to be."

"That part of your life is over with. You've got to go on from here and start living life again, face each day as it comes. Enjoy life. That's what it's all about."

"What you're saying makes sense, but what if Paul tracks me down when he gets out of prison? What if he hates me for that terrible night? For deserting him?"

"You can't do anything about it now, can you? Face that problem when and if it happens. You could spend the rest of your life worrying about the things that will probably never happen. Or you can enjoy each day as if there were no tomorrow."

"Yeah, tomorrow never gets here, does it?"

"Never has in all the years I've lived."

"Oh, Bolt, you've made me feel better, just like Paul used to do. I think I'm falling in love with you." Impulsively, she threw her arms around Bolt's neck, hugged him tight.

Bolt felt the dampness of her tears on his cheek as she brushed against him. Her robe had fallen open when she moved and now the smooth silkiness of her nightgown rubbed against his bare chest. The scent of her clean hair, her flowery perfume, made Bolt giddy.

He tipped her head back with his fingers, kissed her gently on the lips. Heat surged to his loins. His manhood began to expand under the sheet. He wrapped his arms around her, drew her closer to him. She didn't pull away from him.

"I think you're right," she said. "Enjoy each day as it comes."

"You'll be a lot happier that way."

"What I'm trying to say is . . . I want you, Bolt. I

want you to take me. Now. Before I change my mind."

"You sure?"

"Yes. I've never known another man except my husband, but I've been so lonesome."

"As you said this afternoon, it isn't natural for a man to go without sex. Well, it isn't natural for a woman, either."

"I realize that now. I need you. I want to feel you inside me. I want you to make love to me." She pushed Bolt's head back on the pillow, followed him down and lavished him with wet kisses.

Bolt reached up and felt her soft pneumatic breast under the silky fabric of her nightgown. He slipped his hand inside the top of the gown, cupped the bare creamy breast in his hand, kneaded the nipple until it stiffened to a rigid nubbin.

Her hand slid under the sheet, moved down across his bare chest where she encountered the cloth barrier of his shorts. Her fingers quickly worked their way underneath the shorts, found the growing mass of his manhood. She touched it tentatively, at first, then took it in her hand and squeezed it. She moved her hand up and down its pulsing length, felt it stiffen and throb with her touch.

Bolt rolled her over so they were both on their sides, facing each other. She didn't let go of his shaft when he moved her. When they were settled in the new position, she began stroking it again.

Bolt kissed her hard, drove his tongue into her puckered mouth, dipped it in and out of the damp warmth. She responded, opened her mouth wider to accept his playful tongue.

While he was kissing her, he moved his hand away

from her breast, reached down and pulled her night-gown up. He ran his hand up her leg, her thigh, settled it on the furry mound of her sex.

She gasped when he touched her there.

He rubbed his hand around in a circle, plunged his finger inside, felt the damp heat that radiated from her honeypot. His finger became drenched in the fluids of her desire.

"I want you, Bolt. Now. Please put it inside me."

The bed squeaked again as they quickly removed their unneeded garments. It groaned when Lucy lay back on the bed and Bolt positioned himself above her. She spread her legs wide to receive him.

Bolt lowered himself until the tip of his cock touched her wet pussylips.

She gasped again, moaned in ecstasy.

At the very same time, there was a loud thump on the wall that was right next to the bed.

Bolt tensed, frozen in position. He listened carefully.

"What was that?" he whispered.

"Probably Sybil turning over in her sleep," Lucy whispered back.

"Think she can hear us?"

"No. Once she gets to sleep, fireworks could go off in her room and she'd never wake up. Besides, the walls aren't that thin."

Sybil cursed under her breath.

She hadn't meant to eavesdrop in the first place. She only meant to listen long enough to find out who was in Bolt's room, to determine if he was in trouble. When Lucy had started talking about her past, Sybil couldn't stop listening. She even shed a tear when she heard Lucy talk about her husband and that terrible incident that happened five years ago.

She had tried to tune the voices out when she realized the couple in the next room were becoming intimate. Instead, when she heard the bed squeak and groan, she moved closer so she could hear better. In the darkness, she misjudged her distance from the wall and banged her head against it.

She held her breath, then sighed with relief when she heard Lucy say that she was not a light sleeper. It would be a terrible thing to be caught listening in on something so personal.

Sybil was jealous and she knew it. She felt sorry for Lucy now that she knew her circumstances. She was even glad that Lucy was about to experience some sexual pleasure. But why did it have to be with Bolt?

Sybil wanted Bolt for herself. Her pussy dampened and throbbed with the need to have Bolt do the things to her that he was doing with Lucy. She wished she could be the one to share his bed. She had planned to pay him a visit that night but when she went to bed she saw no light under his door. She didn't even know he was back from town.

As she lay perfectly still, listening for the telltale noises from next door, Sybil slid her hand down between her legs. She was so hot, it was all she could do to relieve herself.

It would have to do until the time came when Bolt was making love to her the way he was with Lucy at that very moment.

Chapter Six

Lucy was like a wild animal beneath him, bucking and thrashing like there was no tomorrow. It was as if she had to cram a lifetime of pleasure into the space of a few precious moments. Wildly passionate, she thrust her hips up to meet him with each deep stroke.

She was like a prisoner released from her own body, exorcising her fears, her doubts, her guilt, pounding them to death with her forceful thighs.

And yet, at times, she was like a young girl again, exploring her newly discovered sexuality. Abandoning all inhibitions, she rolled her hips up and down, swallowing his shaft with her steaming love vessel, tightening her muscles around it to keep him deep inside. Mindless with passion, she mumbled endearments in his ear with her hot breath. She ran her wet tongue around his sensitive ear, grabbed his buttocks with both hands and drew him tight to her curvaceous body.

Suddenly, she threw her head back on the pillow and moaned. Her mouth fell open as she tensed and waited for the orgasm that rocked her body with shoots of pleasure.

"Stop a minute," she cried. "I'm coming, I'm coming!"

Bolt waited a minute then began his attack again. He penetrated her again and again, plunging into her steaming depths. She moved with him, matching his rhythm stroke for stroke.

He felt the itch of desire deep in his groin, knew that he was about to spill his seed. Increasing his rhythm, he stroked her hard and deep, burying his shaft to the hilt. He sank into her one last time and let the universe explode around him as his seed burst into the velvet folds of her honeypot.

"Thank you, Bolt," she said a little while later as they lay together on the narrow bed. "You have made me feel like a woman again. I'll always be grateful to you for that. You're a very special person, you know."

He drew her into his arms, kissed her tenderly.

"You're pretty special, too," he said.

"You really mean that, don't you?"

"Yes," he smiled. "And don't ever forget that you're a woman. A very beautiful and desirable woman."

Her fingers were like a feather brushing across his bare chest, his stomach, his inner thighs.

"You know something, Bolt," she sighed. "I'm glad we found each other. I'm your woman now and you are my man."

Her words bit into him like a vise. Clutching at his throat, tightening. Constricting. Strangling. His smile faded away in the darkness. How could he tell her that he couldn't be anybody's man? She might take it real personal if he tried to explain that he wasn't the settling kind. Not yet, he wasn't. How could he destroy the woman, strip her of her new-found dignity and self respect? How could he say any of these things without hurting her?

"Yes, Lucy. For right now, for this very minute, we belong to each other."

"And that's all we have, isn't it? This very minute."

"Yes . . . but things change . . ."

"Don't panic," she laughed, her voice bright and tinkly. "I only meant we have each other for right now. I didn't mean to make it sound like a lifetime commitment. You've made me very happy and nobody can take that away from me. Now, speaking of changes, I've got to get out of here." She scooted to the edge of the bed, fumbled on the floor for her nightgown and robe.

"I wish you could stay longer."

"It would never do if I fell asleep in here. What would the girls think of me if they saw me sneaking out of your room in the morning?"

"They might think you were finally human," he laughed.

Lucy snatched the pillow from under his head, slapped it down on him in mock anger.

"I don't give a damn if they know I slept with you," she said, "but I sure as hell ain't gonna tell them how good you were."

"Why's that?"

"Why, they'd be lined up at your door, two-deep. I'd never get another lick of work out of them."

Bolt tossed the pillow at her as she walked across the room. It hit the door just as she closed it behind her.

He settled down on the bed, listened to her faint footsteps pad along the hall, away from his room, down the stairs where they faded out completely.

A minute later, he heard something else. The squeaking sound of the bed in the next room, as if someone had turned over in their sleep. Then he heard Sybil cough, clear the husk from her voice. The cough was not very loud, but it sounded like she was right next to him. The wall was thinner than he thought.

He knew then that she had heard everything.

Calvin Rader was up unusually early the following morning, soaking his tar-covered hand in hot water. He had managed to pluck all of the chicken feathers out of the tar the night before, but he hated the sight of his black hand. When the heat got so bad he couldn't stand it any more, he raised his hand out of the pot of water on the cookstove, placed it on a towel in his lap. He hunched over, grimaced in pain as he peeled a tiny strip of tar from the back of his hand.

He had been at it for almost an hour and in that time, he had managed to remove only a small circle of tar, about an inch across, from the raw, tender flesh. Each sliver of tar that came off brought new pain and a deeper hatred of Bolt.

He dipped his hand again into the hot water, stood it as long as he could, then brought it out and started to pluck at the repulsive tar.

"What are you doing up so early?" Madge Rader asked her husband when she entered the kitchen wearing a long, sweeping, blue robe. The color of it made her green eyes look blue. Her long red hair had been thoroughly brushed before she came downstairs.

Calvin glanced up and resented her for looking so beautiful that early in the morning.

"Trying to get this damned tar off my hand. What the hell do you think I'm doing?"

She lowered her head, clamped her lips tight to keep from returning Calvin's sarcasm. She hated it when he yelled at her that way. She always retaliated by turning into a nagging wife. She didn't know when their marriage had gone sour but they seemed to be at each other's throats constantly lately. Maybe it was the money that was at the root of their problems. Her money. Maybe he felt less of a man because she had bought the mercantile store for him with money she had before they were married. It was a subject he brought up often enough when his temper flared.

Madge knew that Bolt's arrival in town was at the bottom of their present ill tempers, but for different reasons. Since she had learned of Bolt's presence in Angel's Camp, she had thought of little else. Fear dominated her thoughts, her actions, her emotions. She wouldn't be able to think clearly until Bolt was gone out of her life forever.

"Can I help you?" she asked softly, afraid to trust her own voice.

"I can do it myself," he snapped. "You never help me anyway. I have to do everything myself."

"That's not fair, Calvin," she said, trying to contain her anger. "I do help you."

"If you're talking about your goddamned money again, forget it. I'm tired of you lording it over me that we're living on your money."

"You think the sheriff has arrested that man yet?" she said, avoiding using Bolt's name.

"I hope to hell he has." Calvin jerked when he tore another piece of tar from his hand.

"You've got to make sure of it, Calvin. We can't have men like that in our town."

"No skin off your nose. I'm the one who's hurt. Not you."

"Well, poor you." The sarcasm seeped into the tone of her voice. "You didn't get that awful whorehouse closed down yet, did you? I thought you were going to prove that you were a big man by cleaning up this town."

"Don't push me, Madge."

"Who else am I going to push? You're the head of the Association. The women of this town want a decent place to live. If you and your men can't handle it, we'll do it ourselves."

Calvin glared at Madge. He got up, threw the towel down, stormed out of the kitchen. He went upstairs, finished dressing for work, fished a glove from his dresser drawer. Without telling Madge goodbye, he walked out of the house, slammed the door behind him. He had an hour before he had to be at his store to open it for business, but he was glad to get away from the new pressures his wife was putting on him.

As he walked to the stable, he slipped his black hand into the glove. He saddled his horse, headed out to Dave Talbot's place.

Talbot lived out in the country in an old abandoned farm house that he had bought for a song. The friendship between Rader, Dave Talbot and Pete Booker went back several years, when they were all considered con men by some people they dealt with. In fact when Calvin had married Madge, the other two teased him about marrying the beautiful Madge for her money, using his conning abilities to lure her into his bed. It wasn't true and he resented their crude remarks.

Dave and Pete worked for Rader now and since business was not good enough yet to support their salaries, he paid them with money that belonged to Madge. She didn't think the business could justify the cost of hiring two employees and at times when she was in one of her moods, she would complain bitterly about paying the two men who did nothing to earn their money.

While Pete lived in a modest house in town, Dave lived out in the country in an old abandoned farm house that he had bought for a song. There were no close neighbors near Dave and it was a place he could raise hell when he wanted to. Dave lived alone except for a sixteen-year-old Chinese girl named Lin Wing who served as his house maid, but Rader knew she did more than clean Dave's house and cook his meals.

Lin Wing answered the door when Rader knocked.

"Is Dave home?" Rader asked.

"He still in bed. He vely sick."

"His hand?"

"I take care of hand. His face cut. His head hurt. You want to see him?"

"Yes."

"Come in. He in bedroom."

Even though the bedroom door was open, Rader knocked before he went in.

"What in the hell happened to you?" he said when he saw Dave's puffy face, the cut on his chin.

"Tangled with one of them strangers last night."

"Bolt?"

"Naw. His partner, Penrod. I was in the Dry Creek mindin' my own business when him and some fuckin' miners attacked me."

"Were you drinking again, Dave?"

"Damn right I was drinkin' but it was only to kill the pain." He nodded toward his bandaged hand.

"Your hand any better?"

"Hurts like hell. Broken wrist bones, I'm sure. Lin Wing put a splint on it last night. What the hell you wearing that glove for?"

Rader didn't answer. He moved closer to the bed, spoke in a hushed voice.

"Did you send for that gunny?"

"Yeah. He'll be here Friday, tomorrow afternoon."

"Good. Madge is giving me a hard time."

"So what's new about that?"

"None of your remarks, Dave."

"I don't think we should wait until Hardy Bragg gets here. Let's do 'em in now. Can't you get Booker to take care of them? Or do it yourself?"

"I told you I didn't want any of us involved. We have to wait for an outside man. It's only one more day to wait. You have to be patient."

"Patience my ass!"

"Listen, Dave, you won't be much use to me at the store today. You'd better stay in bed and take it easy."

"I'd planned to."

"I'll check with the sheriff, see if he found out anything about Bolt."

"You do that, Cal." Talbot didn't believe in doing things by the book. Most of the time he went along with Rader because Rader was his meal ticket, but he didn't give a damn about that now. He burned with hatred for

66

the man who had busted his hand. He hated both of them for making him look like an ass. He wasn't going to wait for no asshole sheriff to put the cuffs on Bolt. He wasn't even going to wait for Bragg to get there. He was going to take matters into his own hands. If Rader didn't like it, tough shit.

After Rader left, Talbot got out of bed, dressed himself with one hand. He took his Remington six-shooter from the nightstand, put a handful of bullets in each pocket. Outside, he walked out behind the barn where the bales of hay were stacked. He'd spent many hours there, practicing his target shooting. He would spend many more, learning to shoot again.

Dave set the pistol down on the top of a barrel, dumped the bullets near the gun. Using only his left hand, he managed to jam six bullets into the chamber, cock the hammer back. He took up a stance, aimed at a spot on one of the bales. Feeling clumsy, he squeezed the trigger. The Remington bucked in his hand. The shot was way off. High and to the right.

The weapon was awkward in his left hand and it took him too long to find his coordination. He thumbed the hammer back again, took aim, allowing for the difference between his line of sight in using his left hand instead of the other one. He shot again, was too far to the left. He had overcorrected.

He shot four more times, cursed when he couldn't narrow in on his target. He set the Remington back down on the barrel, put it to half cock. He opened the loading gate, spun the cylinder around, pushed the ejector rod which split the casing out. It wasn't easy. Handling the six-shooter with one hand like that. When the other shells had been ejected, he fed the new bullets in, one at a time.

He did better with the next six shots, missed the imaginary bull's-eye by inches instead of feet. By the third round, he knew he could do it. Right now he needed a drink to help his hangover, but if he practiced all afternoon, he'd be ready by morning.

It would give him great satisfaction to kill Bolt and his friend. Then maybe people would respect him.

Chapter Seven

Sybil Childs had been watching the stairway all morning. Finally, when she heard Bolt's footsteps upstairs, she moved over to the banister, ran her hand across the smooth polished wood, trying to act casual.

"Good morning, Bolt," she said when he came into view.

Bolt bounced down the stairs, a cheerful spring to his steps.

"Morning, Sybil." He smiled at her, saw the knowing twinkle in her bright blue eyes. He liked the natural look of her face without the heavy makeup she wore when she worked. She looked fresh and clean in her gingham dress that buttoned up to her neck. The long, full-skirted frock was tight enough in the bodice to show off her ample bosom.

When he reached the bottom of the steps, she moved in front of him, blocking his way.

"You have a good sleep last night?" she said.

"As a matter of fact, I did. How about yourself?" Bolt brushed on past her, headed for the large front room of the bordello.

Sybil turned, caught up to him.

"It could have been better," she cooed. The way she said it left no doubt in his mind what she meant.

The other girls at the bordello swarmed around him when he entered the room, competing for his attention. Giggling and talking all at once, they reminded him of a flock of chickens at feeding time as they followed him to the couch. Sybil sat down next to him, nuggled as close as she could. Tess sat on his other side as the other girls nudged each other, jostling for position.

They adored him. He was the first man to treat them like fine ladies. Already, through his efforts, they had received a generous increase in pay and that morning, Lucy had given each of them a twenty-dollar bonus so they could buy proper daytime dresses. They were excited because that afternoon they were going to go out and become part of society. The six girls had already decided to split up into pairs to do their shopping, eat at the small cafe.

Lucy was jealous when she entered the room and found Bolt surrounded by the attentive girls. She marched over to the couch, jammed her hands on her hips as she stood before them.

"I told you girls Bolt was a guest in this house. Save your charm for the paying customers." Lucy glared at Sybil when she spoke.

Protesting mildly, all the girls stood up except Sybil who frowned at Lucy, then leaned over and kissed Bolt on the cheek before she got up and left the room with the others.

Bolt enjoyed the attention of the girls at the bordello, but he decided it was time to move out. Although he was attracted to Lucy, he sensed the tension, the jealousy between her and Sybil. Jealous women scared the hell out of him. Especially when they became possessive and smothering. He did not want to become involved with Lucy or the girls to any great degree. He knew he had to convince the town that the bordello was a necessary part of the society. Right now that was more important than staying there and being fussed over by a bunch of giddy girls.

"Lucy, are you being a mite too hard on them girls? They didn't mean anything by sitting with me. They're just excited about their shopping expedition."

"I know. It's just that I don't want them to be a bother to you. Heaven knows, they could take up all your time if you let them."

"Well, I've decided to move into the hotel for a few days. Tom's staying at the Angels Hotel. I'll take a room there."

Bolt saw the sad look on Lucy's face.

"But, Bolt, you can't . . ."

"Look, if Rader and Talbot are gunning for me, and likely they are after yesterday, I don't want them coming here to do their shooting. If I stay at the hotel, it might keep the pressure off you for awhile. Somehow, we've got to convince the townspeople to keep the bordello open and I think I can do it better if I'm in town."

"But I'll miss you," she said lowering her head.

"Hey, this isn't goodbye. I'll be around." He chucked her under the chin, gave her a brief kiss.

"You'd better. Do you want me to go up to your room with you and help you gather your things?" She wriggled her hips, thrust her loins against him, gave him a sultry look.

"Not now, you shameless hussy," he laughed, giving her a swat on the rear end. "But I'll be back. I promise."

Bolt sipped coffee from a mug as he waited for Tom to join him for supper in the dining room of the Angels Hotel. He had already checked into a room and talked to Tom.

As he glanced around the room at the other diners, his eyes settled on the woman who sat alone at the next table. She was staring at him, but turned away quickly. Bolt studied her for a moment, fascinated by her plain beauty. She wore a simple dark blue dress with three rows of white cording around the long sleeves, the collar and a few inches above the hemline of the long skirt. Her matching hat, which had only one row of white cording around the wide brim, shielded her eyes when she turned away from him.

The next time he looked at her, he had a chance to glimpse her haunting hazel eyes before she looked away. He tried hard not to look at her again, but it became a compulsion to glance over and catch her staring at him. Finally, his curiosity got the best of him. He pushed his chair out, stepped over to her table.

"Pardon me, ma'am, do I know you?"

She looked up, startled by his voice. Her eyes were even more haunting than they had seemed.

"No, I don't think so," she said politely.

"You appeared to be staring at me. I thought maybe we'd met. Or do I have dirt on my face?" He brushed his cheek, wiped an imaginary smudge away.

"I'm Alexis Townsend, the schoolmarm for Angel's

Camp." Her smile was polite, but guarded. "I attended the public meeting of the Merchants Association yesterday afternoon. Aren't you the one who stopped them from torturing that prostitute?"

"Yeah. Does that make me the bad guy?"

"No. Not at all, Mister . . . uh."

"Bolt. Jared Bolt."

"Won't you sit down, Mister Bolt?" She pushed her empty plate away, pulled her coffee mug closer.

"Just for a minute. I'm waiting for a friend." He snatched his own coffee mug from his table, sat down across from her.

"I was very impressed by your actions. You don't know how horrified I was when I saw what they were going to do to that poor girl. You were very brave to stand up to Calvin Rader like that. Not many around here who would."

"Not brave, miss. I just couldn't stand there and watch them abuse an innocent girl just because she happened to be a harlot. Being a schoolmarm, you probably don't agree that a harlot can be considered innocent."

"Oh, I do agree. She's a woman, after all, and no man has a right to abuse any of us, no matter how we conduct our personal lives."

"You sound pretty liberal for a schoolmarm."

"I'm surprised at you, Mister Bolt." Her eyes seemed to darken.

"Why? What'd I do?"

"Judging a woman by her position in life, like all the other men I know. I thought you might be different."

"I just meant . . ."

"I may be an old maid schoolmarm, but I am not

73

prim and stuffy. I'm not against prostitution, as such. I think prostitutes play a necessary part in our society. The people of this town were perfectly willing to have this outlet for men's passions until Madge Rader started hounding her husband to close down Lucy's Place."

Bolt's eyes widened when he heard Madge's name mentioned again. It was not a common name. He wondered if it could be the same Madge he knew a few years back. Madge Garrett. That was her name.

"Do you know Madge Rader?" he asked.

"Heavens, no. I've never seen her. I hear she sticks pretty close to home except when she attends social events and since we don't move in the same circles, I've not met her. Some say she's a recluse. Others think she's afraid to leave the house."

"Do you know what she looks like?"

"From what I hear, she's a very striking woman. Very cultured and elegant, but you couldn't prove it by me."

That didn't help Bolt. He shook his head.

"You know her maiden name?"

"No."

"Know how long she's been married to Rader?"

"No, but I might be able to find out. I have a cousin in San Francisco who used to know Madge."

"How long would it take you to find out?"

"If I sent a message by telegraph, I might be able to get a reply by tomorrow afternoon when the stage arrives."

"It would help. Alexis, you know the townspeople better than I do. How can I convince them to keep the bordello open?"

"I think most of them are already convinced. It's Rader and the Merchants Association who are causing the problem."

"Then how do I deal with them without resorting to bloodshed?"

"Go around them."

"How?"

"Call your own meeting. Invite the people of Angel's Camp . . ." She stopped talking when she saw the tall, tousled-haired man standing at their table.

"Invite the people to what?" grinned Tom Penrod. "You having a party, Bolt?"

"Oh, Alexis, this is my friend, Tom Penrod. Tom, this is Alexis Townsend, local schoolmarm. Pull up a chair, Tom."

"Did I miss supper?" Tom pulled out a chair, plunked his lean frame down.

"No, we were just talking about having a town meeting. But I think it would take too long to organize it. We would have to let everyone know."

"You could put fliers up all over town," Alexis offered.

"But we don't have much time. I think Rader and his men are going to push pretty hard. I have a feeling if we don't get the townspeople on our side by tomorrow, we can expect trouble."

"You can do it," Alexis said. "I know a printer who works for the newspaper, Scotty McDoogle. He's printed up some quiz papers for me and I think he could do a rush job for you."

"In time to have the meeting, say, tomorrow afternoon? Think that would give him enough time?"

"Tomorrow is Friday. Yes, I think so. If you give him

the information tonight, he could get it all set up and run it first thing in the morning. Once he starts printing, it wouldn't take him more than an hour to print the fliers."

"Good. If he can do it, we'll set it for tomorrow afternoon, about two o'clock. Tom, do you think you can handle it for me?"

"Right now?"

"No, after supper."

Alexis pushed back from the table, leaned down to retrieve her pocketbook from beside her chair and stood up.

"While you two are eating, I'll go across the street to the stage stop office and send that telegram," she said.

"Will you come back?"

"Yes, I'll be back."

After she was gone, Tom and Bolt ordered beef stew, biscuits and honey, a bottle of red wine. Bolt asked the waiter for a pencil and when he brought it, Bolt took one of the linen napkins from the table, wrote out the information for the flier.

"You work fast, don't you?" Tom said as he sopped the stew juice up with a biscuit.

"We have to, Tom. I don't trust Rader. Not a peep out of him today, but he's got something up his sleeve."

"I didn't mean Rader. I meant your lady friend. She's a purty one. Wouldn't mind having her in my bed at night."

"Just remember, she's a schoolmarm."

"They got needs too. Besides, maybe she could teach me something new." Tom grinned, wiped his mouth with his napkin and pushed his plate away.

"Yeah. Some manners maybe. You'd put the boots

to anything that wore a skirt."

"Hell, they don't have to wear a skirt for me. I ain't that particular. Only problem with this town is it's only got one whorehouse. I can go through them girls in a day."

"If we don't stop Rader, there won't even be one whorehouse."

"You know that Talbot feller is plumb crazy. He's the one to watch out for."

Alexis returned just then, said she had sent the message to her cousin.

"Would you like a glass of wine?" Bolt asked.

"That would be nice."

Bolt ordered another glass, poured the wine. He handed her the linen napkin he had scribbled on.

"Take a look at this," he said. "That look all right to you?"

Bolt watched her read his notes and again, he couldn't take his eyes off her. She was startlingly beautiful in simple blue dress and the hat that held her sleek brown hair in a bun. He noticed that her nose was slightly upturned and her long dark lashes emphasized her big hazel eyes.

She laughed and her voice was like a soft tinkling bell. He noticed something else about her, too. She had dimples when she smiled. Bolt was a sucker for dimples.

"What's so funny?" he asked.

"The information you wrote down is perfect for the flier. The only thing is, you don't say where it's going to be held."

"Small detail. Where would you suggest?"

"The town hall or the Angel Community Church."

"The town hall," Bolt said. He added the information to the napkin, handed it to Tom.

"Can you take care of it, Tom? Tell McDoogle we need a hundred fliers. Here's ten bucks. If it's any more than that, I'll pay him in the morning."

"Where do I find this McDoogle character?" Tom asked.

After Alexis gave him directions, Tom pulled his wiry hulk out of the chair, slid his hat onto his head, squared it off and departed.

Alexis sipped from her glass of wine, looked at Bolt over the brim of the glass.

"Would you care to walk me home?" she asked. "I don't live very far from here."

Desire surged into Bolt's loins when he looked into her large doe eyes. She looked so innocent, so prim and proper. He wondered if she knew what she was doing by inviting him to her home. He took a deep breath, made his decision.

"Maybe I shouldn't," he said.

He felt her warm hand press against his thigh under the table.

"Maybe you should," she said in a low throaty voice.

Bolt no longer wondered if she knew what she was doing.

Chapter Eight

Alexis lived two short blocks from the Angels Hotel. Actually she lived on the street just behind the main part of town but it took two blocks of walking to get there.

"Nice quiet neighborhood," Bolt said as Alexis was unlocking her door.

Alexis stepped inside, lit the coal-oil lantern just inside the door.

"Yes. I like it that way. The couple next door are elderly. They go to bed with the chickens so I never hear any noise from them. The publisher of the Angel Gazette lives a few doors down and there's a boarding-house on the corner. All pleasant people. Mister Booker lives in the house across the street, but I don't think he stays there half the time."

"Booker lives there?" Bolt's eyebrows raised as he glanced at the darkened house across the street. "The same Mister Booker who was holding Sybil Childs at the tar and feathering?"

"Yes. He works for Rader, you know. I lost my

respect for him when I saw him holding on to her but I suppose he thought he was doing his civic duty. I've never had any quarrel with him. He's always been pleasant to me in the store and he's certainly never caused any disturbance around here.

"Do you know anything about him?"

"Only that he works at the Mercantile Store. People tend to mind their own business around here."

"Not so I'd noticed."

"You're right. Come in, Bolt. Please." After Bolt, stepped inside, she closed and locked the door.

The room smelled of her lavender perfume and as she walked across the floor and lit another lantern on the fireplace mantel, Bolt saw the influence of her femininity in the decor. Colorful velvet throw pillows adorned the couch and heavy floral-print curtains covered the windows. The paintings on the wall were of ballerinas and still life flowers and the bookcases contained as many knickknacks as books. A neat stack of school papers sat on the roll-top desk in the corner of the room.

The spotless room took on a soft glow when Alexis lit a large candle on the coffee table.

"Would you like some brandy?" she asked.

"Sounds good."

"It's in the china cabinet. So are the glasses. Would you do the honors while I get out of this tight dress?" She smiled, turned and walked away, went into the next room where she lit a hand-painted lamp on her dressing table.

Bolt walked to the cabinet that held a full set of good china, cut crystal goblets, two china figurines, a bottle of whiskey and a couple of bottles of liqueurs. He opened the glass door of the cabinet, removed the bottle of brandy and two sparkling brandy snifters with cut glass stems. He carried them back to the coffee table, set them down near the candle.

He poured a small amount of the amber liquid in each glass, picked one up and swirled it around. He held it up to his nose, breathed in, let the biting aroma fill his nostrils. After he took a sip, he picked up the other glass, carried both of them to the bedroom door.

Pausing in the doorway, he saw Alexis sitting at her dressing table wearing only a full white petticoat with narrow shoulder straps. He watched as she unfolded her long dark hair from its tight bun. The lamp light threw shimmering golden streaks across her sleek hair as she ran a brush through the strands.

Desire stabbed at his loins when she set the brush down and slipped the straps of her petticoat down over her smooth shoulders. Without the support of the straps, the lace bodice of her petticoat fell to her waist, exposing creamy white breasts.

He stepped into the bedroom, saw her reflection in the mirror. She looked like a rare delicate statue with her full bare breasts, the dark aureole of her nipples against the white of her skin, the dark hair falling about her face.

His manhood throbbed, began to grow with the blood that raced through his veins.

He moved across the room, stood behind her. She looked up into the mirror and he caught her doe-eye gaze with his own. They stared at each other, made silent promises with their eyes.

Bolt reached his arms around both sides of her shoulders, set the brandy glasses down on the table top.

When he brought his hands back, he stopped at her breasts. He cupped one in each hand, kissed her on the nape of the neck.

"I brought your brandy," he husked.

Alexis shivered with his hot breath at her ear. Her eyes still focused on Bolt's reflection, she took the brandy snifter in her hand, touched it to the mirror. Without shifting her eyes away from his, she took a sip, haunted him with her sensual mirror image.

He kneaded her breasts, felt her heartbeat quicken. His manhood spasmed involuntarily, stiffened against its cloth prison. He reached over, picked up his own brandy snifter, clinked it to hers. Not once did their eyes lose contact.

"To you, lovely lady."

"To us. Tonight," she said, her voice like soft velvet.

They sipped the brandy, set the snifters back down.

She turned, tilted her head back, waited with moist parted lips for his kiss.

Her lips were soft and pliable under the pressure of his mouth. He took a bare breast in his hand, held her chin with the other as he crushed her mouth with his passionate kiss, his breath coming in short pants. His tongue slid easily into her hot mouth. She responded with her own passion.

He broke the kiss, lifted her from the stool to a standing position. She pushed her petticoat down past her hips, let it fall to the floor in a whisper of rustling cloth. He stepped back, took in her beauty with his eyes. The lamplight bronzed her body with its flicker.

He grabbed her, pulled her into his arms, felt her breasts crush against his chest. He thrust his hips forward, pushed his hardness into her loins.

"Oooooohhhhhhh," she sighed and kissed him again.

Bolt picked her up and carried her to the bed. He quickly stripped out of his clothes, climbed in next to her. His hand found her dark thatch. She spread her legs, encouraged his touch. His shadow flowed across her body as he moved over her, positioned himself between her splayed legs. She arched her back, thrust her thighs up to meet him as he dipped down to touch the pink flesh that was hidden by the nest of hair.

He penetrated her, felt the tight muscles immediately grip his shaft. He eased into the oiled passageway, then sank his member to the steaming pit of her honeypot.

They didn't talk. Their kind of loving didn't need words or whispered expressions of endearment. The only sounds in the room where those of heavy breathing, panting, the slap, slap of bare flesh against flesh. He knew when her orgasm came without her telling him. A man knew these things after a time. Just before she climaxed, she whipped him into a frenzy with her undulating hips, her hands grabbing his hips and pulling him to her with no way of backing out.

He could have lasted longer. He didn't want to. It felt too good to stop and pause. He just kept stroking, let it come naturally.

Even after he stopped spurting and rolled off her body, it was a long time before they spoke.

"You're a good man, Bolt. Even better than I'd dreamed."

"You surprise me, Alexis."

"With my boldness?" She smiled and in the lamp glow, her dimples recessed into darkness. "I'm a woman with normal needs and desires."

"Even schoolmarms have needs," he said idly.

"What's that supposed to mean?" she laughed her musical laugh.

"Just thinking aloud."

"Come on, tell me."

"Just something Tom said tonight."

"He said that? You tell Tom he was right."

They relaxed then, let the dampness dry from their bodies. After a time, Bolt started to get up.

"Where you going?"

"I'd better be going. It wouldn't do to have your elderly neighbors see me leaving at dawn."

"Oh, no you don't." She grabbed his shoulder, pulled him back down on the bed. "I've got you here and I'm not about to let you go until morning. I don't really give a damn what the neighbors think."

Bolt kissed her and knew that he would take her again before the night was over.

It was just after dawn when Pete Booker stepped outside on his porch, closed the door behind him, locked it with his key. He was an early riser and it was his custom to walk the two blocks to the Open Cafe for a leisurely breakfast before reporting to work at the Mercantile Store. That wasn't the name of the cafe, but that was what everybody called it. Only two signs in the window proclaimed it a place to eat. One said "OPEN" and the other said "CAFE" and nobody had bothered to call it anything else.

He walked to the edge of the porch, paused long enough to sniff the crisp morning air. Dawn was his favorite time of day. It gave him a sense of power to watch the early light of morning give life to the dark mysterious forms of darkness. It was as if his presence caused the magical lights to come down from the sky. Sometimes he felt like a ruthless artist, wiping color into the things around him with the stroke of a brush. But these were thoughts best kept to himself.

He stood on the porch longer than usual. It was getting so he didn't look forward to going to work. He didn't like all this business of cleaning up the town and closing the bordello. It wasn't that he really disapproved, but he didn't like the way Rader was going about it. He thought Rader and Talbot and the rest of them were making too big a deal about the bordello. He didn't see anything wrong with it and, in fact, had visited it often before Rader began his campaign to close it down. He knew Calvin's wife Madge had pushed him into it, but that didn't make it right just because she didn't approve. Pete knew he had to go along with it if he didn't want to lose his job, but if Rader pulled any more stunts like tarring and feathering a frightened young harlot, he'd pull up stakes and find another way to make a living.

Pete walked down the steps, looked over at the ominous form of the dark cypress tree in his yard. Even though it was just a tree, it was tall enough to give any man a start in the right light.

He turned, glanced across the street when he heard Alexis Townsend's front door open. It surprised him because it was much too early for her to leave for the one-room schoolhouse where she taught the village children. As his eyes focused in the pale gray of dawn, he saw the dark form appear in the open doorway. Orange light from a lantern inside the house surrounded the dark shape.

When he realized there were two forms in the doorway instead of one, he stepped over to the cypress, ducked behind its thick branches. It wasn't his nature to spy on anyone, but he didn't want to cause Miss Townsend any embarrassment by walking by her house just then.

When he looked over again, he saw the couple kissing. The man turned around, started down the steps. Pete held his breath. As the man headed for the street, Pete squinted his eyes, tried to see who it was. And then he knew. It was Bolt!

Pete had always admired Alexis Townsend, thought of her as virginal. How could she be fooling around with a scoundrel like Bolt? Maybe he had forced his way into her house during the night. But if that was so, why would she be kissing him now? No, she was a willing partner, that was obvious.

Pete stood perfectly still until Bolt had passed by him and Alexis had closed her door.

It took him a moment to get over the shock, but when he did, he knew what he had to do. He went out behind his house, saddled his horse and rode off as the morning sun began its long climb in the east.

His discovery could not wait until he got to work.

Rader had to be told right away.

It was light outside when Bolt entered the Angels Hotel and headed for his upstairs room. He encountered Tom at the foot of the stairs.

"You just getting home?" Tom grinned.

"Yeah, and I got a message for you."

"Who from?"

"Alexis. She said to tell you that, 'Yes. Even school-marms have needs.'"

Tom laughed, slapped Bolt on the back.

"I told you she was horny, you son of a gun."

"What are you doing up at this ungodly hour?"

"I'd tell you I was just getting home, too, but you wouldn't believe me."

"The hell I wouldn't."

"Those fliers you wanted will be ready by nine o'clock. I thought I'd eat breakfast, then go round up some tacks and a hammer. Know where I can get them?"

"I'm sure Calvin Rader sells them in his store."

"I ain't going in there and give that bastard my business. Not if my life depended on it and it probably would. Hell, I'll steal them first."

"Any change left from the ten I gave you?"

"Just enough to pay for my breakfast. If you want to join me, you'll have to pay for your own."

"Tom, did anyone ever tell you you're a prick?"

"You gonna go eat with me or not?"

"Think I will. Now that you mention it, I'm starved."

"She wore you out, did she?"

"You might just be surprised."

They went into the dining room, found a table.

"After breakfast," Bolt said, "I'm going to go up and change clothes then go on over to the bordello to check on the girls, see if they had any trouble last night. You can start distributing those fliers."

"Where do you want me to put them?"

"Everywhere people will see them. Put them in every store, saloon, and place of public thoroughfare. Tack 'em up on every post you see. Stick them in windows. Attach them to saddles. Shove 'em up horses asses. I don't care, just so everyone in town sees them."

"This ain't gonna make Rader and his bunch none too happy."

"Fuck Rader. He doesn't scare me. Oh, and take the fliers around to all the miners. We just may need them to swing things our way."

"Hell, that'll take me all morning. The damned meeting will be over with before I get all of them up."

"I'll help you, Tom, just as soon as I get back from Lucy's Place. I'll catch up to you in town."

"Sure you will. Knowing you, you'll show up just as I'm tacking up the last poster."

"I'll try my damnedest to time it that way."

Chapter Nine

Rader yawned, flexed his muscles, cursed the early hour of the morning. He had been up half the night, peeling the stubborn tar from his fingers and he was about to go at it again. Most of the tar was gone from his fingers and the palm of his hand, but he still had work to do on his thumb and the back of his hand where the skin was more sensitive.

He sat down at the kitchen table, glad that Madge was still asleep. He lowered his hand into the pot of hot water in front of him, brought it right back out when the heat burned the raw flesh where he had already removed the tar.

He cursed again, blotted his hand with the towel. He just couldn't take the pain any more. He'd have to wait a few days until the skin was not so sore and festered.

He got up, walked to the cupboard for some ointment that would soothe the sores on his hand. Something caught his eye as he passed by the window. A shadow of movement. He leaned closer to the window, saw that someone was riding his way. With the low sun at the rider's back, it took Rader a couple of minutes to recognize Pete Booker and his horse.

Something was wrong, he realized. Booker wasn't the type to be paying a social visit this time of the morning. Fact is, Booker seldom rode out to the house at all.

Rader had the door open by the time Booker and his horse reached the front of the house.

"What's the matter?" he called out.

"Good morning, Calvin. Something I thought you should know about right away." Booker dismounted, stepped over to the hitching post with the reins in his hand.

Upstairs, Madge Rader stirred in her sleep, heard the loud voices downstairs. She popped out of bed, dashed to her bedroom window. She pulled the curtain aside, looked down to see Pete Booker tying his horse to the post.

"Damn it, Pete, what is it?" Calvin called impatiently. "Did something happen to Talbot?"

"No, it's Bolt," Pete said as he walked up the steps.

The mention of Bolt's name stabbed at Madge like a knife. As her husband and Pete moved into the house, she tiptoed across her room, stood silently at her open bedroom door, prayed that she would be able to hear them.

"What's he done now?" Rader asked.

"He spent the night at the schoolmarm's house."

"Alexis Townsend? I don't believe it."

"It's true. I saw him with my own eyes. No mistaking who it was or what they were up to. I saw him leave her house at dawn."

"No doubt he forced his attentions on her," said

Calvin as he poured a cup of coffee for his friend, motioned for him to sit down at the kitchen table. "Probably used a gun, or more likely he threatened her with scandal if she didn't give him what he was after."

"Maybe so, but she didn't look like she was complaining about it, the way they was kissing when he left."

"That bastard! He comes here to Angel's Camp and makes himself at home, doesn't he?"

"Appears that way."

"First he tries to push us around, then sticks up for them harlots and now this. Sleeping with Miss Townsend, of all people. What's he trying to prove?"

"I don't know. I just thought you'd want to know."

"Yes, I do. This puts a new light on things. It's an insult to the whole town, having him bully his way around like this. The people won't like it one bit when they find out that Bolt was sleeping with Miss Townsend."

"But she was willing."

"Then she's got to be fired."

"But she's a damned good teacher."

"We can't have the innocent children of this town being influenced by her corrupt mind. I'll see to it personally that she doesn't spend another day in that classroom."

"How you gonna manage that? You don't have the authority to fire her."

"The hell I don't. The Merchant's Association is charged with cleaning up this town and I'm president."

"But you can't act alone. The other members have their say-so."

"According to our rules, in an emergency, I have the

authority to make a decision about such things. But, you've got a good point. We'll present the facts to the Association, get them all fired up. We'll make an example out of Miss Townsend. Let the people know that if they associate with Bolt, they're gonna be outcasts. I'm going to make damned sure that Bolt has a hard way to go."

"Seems to me, if we run Bolt out of town, our problems will be over."

"That's right. I've got the sheriff looking into the matter now." Rader wasn't too worried about getting rid of Bolt. He knew the hired gunman would be there that afternoon, but he didn't want to tell Pete about it. That was something that was just between him and Dave Talbot. Pete was different from Talbot. Dave would jump at any chance to get even with someone, even if it meant killing a man. Pete was not that way. Pete hated violence and he certainly didn't approve of taking the law into his own hands.

"Good. Luke Pettibone should be the one to handle it anyway."

"Yeah, let Luke escort Bolt out of town and we'll take care of the schoolmarm. What I want you to do is notify all the members of the Association that there'll be a special meeting this morning. Say about nine o'clock. Tell 'em to meet at the store." Rader got up from the table. "Thanks for riding out."

Rader walked Pete to the door and when he got back to the kitchen, Madge was standing there in her robe. With her hair already brushed out, she looked beautiful, as she always did early in the morning.

"Good morning, Madge. Did you hear what's going on?"

"Yes. I couldn't help but overhear. Calvin, you've got to get rid of Bolt right away. We can't have men like that around."

"What in the hell do you think I'm doing?" he snapped, annoyed that she had started her nagging already.

"Well, I haven't seen any evidence of it," she said sarcastically, hurt that Calvin had yelled at her. "And that whorehouse has to be shut down right away. Prostitution is bringing in men like Bolt and we women won't stand for it."

"Madge, we're working on it."

"Not fast enough. That whorehouse had better be closed by tonight or you're going to be sorry."

"Are you threatening me?"

"You might say that. I can promise you this. If you don't get rid of Bolt and that filthy whorehouse by tonight, you can forget about the store and me and everything else."

"What do you mean by that?"

"I mean that I'm going to leave you. Without me, you'll have nothing. I own the store. You won't have a dollar to your name if I leave." Madge whirled around, stomped out of the room.

"You and your fuckin' money!" he shouted after her.

Madge ran up the stairs in tears. She hated the fights, knew some of them were her fault. She was so nervous, she wasn't herself. When she had heard the men talking about Bolt sleeping with Alexis Townsend, she was instantly jealous. She didn't know why, after all these years. She had wanted Bolt back then, very much. But he had turned her down and she never got over it. She wished she could tell Calvin about the things that were upsetting her. She wished Calvin would take her in his arms, like he used to do, and make all of her fears go away.

She knew, though, that there were some things about her past she could never tell her husband.

Tom arrived at the newspaper office at nine o'clock to pick up the fliers. The reporter, who was busy at his cluttered desk, told Tom that McDoogle was in the back and Tom could go on back.

"Don't mind the mess back here," McDoogle said when he saw Tom. "We're making this room a little bigger and the carpenters left a mess at quitting time last night. Hope they'll finish up today. I could barely get near the printer this morning with all this stuff piled up around it."

"Are the fliers ready?"

"Yes. I just finished them a few minutes ago." He picked up the stack of posters, handed them to Tom. "Be careful they don't smudge. The ink's not quite dry."

"Thanks for the rush job."

"Any time I can help . . ."

"Do you suppose I could borrow one of those hammers over there?"

McDoogle turned his head, looked at the tools piled in one corner of the room.

"How long would you need it?"

"Shouldn't take me more than an hour to put all these up."

"I reckon it would be all right. The workers aren't here yet and there are three hammers here." He picked one of them up, handed it to Tom. "Sure, go ahead."

"How about tacks? You got any I could buy off you?"

McDoogle rummaged through the rubble, found several small boxes of tacks. He gave one of them to Tom. Tom reached in his pocket, brought out a silver coin, put it in McDoogle's hand.

"They'll probably never miss the tacks," the printer said, "but I'll see they get the money."

"Thanks again. I'll return the hammer when I'm through with it."

Tom took the posters and supplies out to his horse. He kept a handful of fliers out, put everything else in his saddlebag. He would ride out to the miners' shacks first because Bolt wanted to make sure the miners would attend the meeting. Then he would come back and start putting them up all over town. He hoped Bolt would meet him in time to help.

At the same time Tom was picking up the fliers from the printer, Calvin Rader was meeting with the members of the Merchants Association. The dozen men sat in hard, straight-back chairs around the pot-bellied stove, although there was no fire burning. There was no need for one.

Rader explained the purpose of the emergency meeting. He told them about Bolt and Alexis Townsend, exaggerating when he thought it necessary, coloring the tone of his words when he wanted to. He made a mental note of those who went along with his convictions from the beginning and those who had to be convinced.

Pete Booker said nothing during the meeting except

to verify that he had witnessed the incident of Bolt leaving the schoolmarm's home at dawn and, "Yes, they had kissed," when pushed by Rader to tell everything.

Rader had little trouble convincing them to vote his way.

"Who's gonna tell Miss Townsend?" one of the members asked.

"I'll do it," said Rader. "It won't be an easy task, but I think it is my duty as President, to be the spokesman for the group."

Relieved that Rader had offered to tell Miss Townsend she was fired, the others got up and left.

"I told you they would all agree," Rader said to Pete Booker when the others had left. "There was no need for you to worry about it. We're doing the best thing."

"I'm sure as hell glad you're the one who's going to deliver the bad news. I don't think I could face her."

"Let's go see the sheriff. Maybe he's got some news about Bolt by now. Tommy can handle the store while we're gone."

Leaving the young cleanup boy in charge, Rader and Booker walked down to the sheriff's office, which was two doors away from Rader's Mercantile Store.

Luke Pettibone didn't get up out of his chair when Rader and Booker walked in. He knocked the ashes off his cigar, waited for one of them to speak.

"Find out anything about Bolt yet?"

"Yes and no," said the sheriff, not seeming too concerned about Rader's problems.

"What's that supposed to mean?"

"In reply to the telegram I sent yesterday, I got a telegram in return that said Bolt was a wanted man, that there was a wanted poster out on him a few years back. Seems like you were right about him being an outlaw."

"Then why in the hell haven't you arrested him?" Rader boomed, his face flushed with anger.

"'Cause I don't know what he's wanted for. And since it's been so long, that matter may have been cleared up already."

"Can't you arrest him anyway, hold him in jail until you have more information?"

"Things don't work that way, Rader. I can't just go out there and arrest him because you tell me to. I have to have something to charge him with when I arrest him. That's what justice is all about."

"Your reputation's on the line, Pettibone," Rader threatened. "You haven't been sheriff of Angel's Camp more than a couple of months and you're gonna find that you'd better go along with the citizens or you won't have a job."

"Threats aren't necessary, Rader. They won't change my thinking. As long as I'm sheriff, we do things my way. I looked through all the old files here and couldn't come up with a wanted poster on Bolt. But, you'll be happy to know, I did send my deputy up to Jackson to find out why Bolt was wanted. The sheriff up there has every poster that was ever printed. I should have some answers for you later today if you'd care to check back."

"Why the hell should I have to check back with you?" Rader fumed. "You're the sheriff here. Just do the job you're paid to do. And you'd better move a hell of a lot faster than you have been or your job will be under consideration at the next Merchants Association meeting."

"Good day, gentlemen," Pettibone said. He puffed

on his cigar, blew the smoke straight across the desk so it swirled around Rader's face. He watched the two men turn and leave his office. When they were gone, he leaned forward in his chair, snubbed the cigar out in the ashtray. He hated bullies like Calvin Rader and worse, he hated to buckle under to that type of high-handed pressure. But he was going to have to take action soon because he knew Rader meant what he said. He knew his job was on the line and he knew Rader carried enough power to carry through with his threat.

Only one thing he feared more. And that was the idea of facing Bolt. He knew damned well why Bolt was a wanted man. He killed two lawmen a few years back. The telegraph had told him that much. He had sent his deputy to Jackson to pick up a copy of the wanted poster. It would give him the proof he wanted. But more than that, it was a way of stalling. Until that poster came back, he had a legitimate excuse to put off confronting Bolt with the accusation. He hoped his deputy took his time. Maybe things would work themselves out and he'd never have to face Bolt.

Chapter Ten

Tom made a quick swing by the miners' shacks that were scattered along the countryside. He handed out fliers to those who were still at their shacks, rode out to the diggings to distribute them to the miners who were already working.

When he rode up to one of the claims, he saw Hard Luck Hal stooped over a small stream, sloshing water around in a gold pan. Chester and Dinger carried buckets of water to the nearby sluice box where they dumped the water into the highest end of the wooden box.

Wiley stood over the sluice box, watched for the small gold particles that would settle to the bottom and be caught by wooden riffles. Clem stood near the arrastre where a mule was harnessed to the rock crusher. The mule walked around and around in the small circle, goaded on by Clem's occasional shouts.

"You having any luck?" Tom called out from his saddle after he had watched the operation for a few minutes.

Hard Luck Hal turned his head toward Tom. When he saw Tom, he set his pan down on the ground, got up.

"Hello there, Tom. Not much luck so far today. A little dust, that's all. We ain't hit pay dirt, I can tell you that. What brings you out this way?" He walked over to Tom.

"Just brought you some fliers." Tom handed one down to Hard Luck Hal.

The grizzled miner laughed when he took the sheet of paper.

"I thought you said fryers. I thought maybe you was bringin' us some chicken for lunch."

Tom wondered how Hal could eat chicken with half of his teeth missing. The four other miners stopped what they were doing, crowded around Tom. He handed down one flier for each of them.

"Son of a gun," hooted Hal when he had finished reading it. "About time someone stuck up to those phony bastards who are tryin' to rule everybody's life."

Dinger stared at his flier, a blank expression on his face. "What does it say?" he finally asked.

"Dinger, when you gonna learn yourself to read?" Hard Luck Hal said. "Bolt's having a meetin' this afternoon and we're invited. He says it's for improvin' the town and discussin' issues. It's at two o'clock at the town hall."

"Hope all you fellows can make it," Tom said.

"We'll be there," Hard Luck Hal assured him. "I wouldn't miss it for anything."

"Good. See you there." Tom wished he had time to watch them work, but he had to get back and get the posters up in town.

When he got back, he stopped his horse at one end of

the main street, figuring to go up one side of the street, come back the other side. He dismounted, took the posters, hammer and tacks out of his saddle bag, closed it back up. He worked fast, tacking fliers everywhere he could. He put them on porch posts, next to the doors of businesses, on hitch rails. He stuck some in store windows, handed them out to passersby.

When he neared the Mercantile Store, he hesitated, then tacked one of the posters on the door of the store. He expected Rader or one of his men to come bursting out of the building with a shotgun in hand, but it went without a hitch. Tom peered in the window as he walked by the Mercantile, but it was brighter outside than in and all he could see was his own reflection. He walked on, tacked notices up on the next building. And when he reached the next building, he hesitated again. The sign out front said "Sheriff." Tom supposed there was no law against putting a public notice on the sheriff's place, so he tacked one on a post near the front door.

He continued on down the street, plastering everything with the white posters. When he reached the end of the buildings, he crossed the street and started back up the other side. He was almost finished and there was no sign of Bolt. But then he hadn't figured Bolt would show until the work was done.

Ten minutes later, he was nearing the end of the street where he had left his horse. Three more buildings to cover and he'd be through.

The sun felt good on his back as he faced the small building with the sign that read, "Sam Ackroyd— Barber—Surgeon." He held the poster up to the post in front of the barber shop, positioned it, stuck a tack in it, then drew back the hammer to tap it in place.

An icy chill went up Tom's spine as he felt the dark shadow flow across his back. Someone was behind him. Someone who had snuck up silently, unannounced.

Without taking time to think, and without turning around, Tom swung the hammer down hard, brought it up in a powerful swing behind him. He heard the scuffle of feet as the ambusher jumped back. Tom started to whirl around, froze when a shot rang out. The bullet whizzed by his ear, close enough so Tom felt the force of air against one cheek. He dropped to the ground, scampered for cover. The blast had rendered him temporarily deaf and he could hear nothing around him except a loud ringing in his ears.

Bolt rode up a dirt road, hoping he would be in time to help Tom with the posters. He had spent more time at the bordello than he had planned. Lucy reported that there had been no further trouble there and she gave Bolt credit for that. The tension was still there. Between Lucy and Sybil. He saw them glaring at each other when he talked to them.

As he was leaving the bordello, the other girls swarmed around him, each anxious to tell him about their shopping expedition. They were so excited about it, he took the time to listen to each of them tell her story. One of them said things had gone so well, they were thinking about going to church on Sunday. He told them if that's what they wanted to do, they should do it and not be intimidated by any remarks or stares that came their way.

He finally had managed to break away from the girls

without hurting their feelings and was on his way to help Tom. He turned the corner, entered the main street.

The spatterings of fresh white posters on all the posts and building fronts caught his eye immediately. Tom had done a good job. As he rode down the street, he saw the poster in front of the Mercantile Store, chuckled to himself. Tom had a great sense of humor.

He rode further, finally spotted Tom near the end of the block, in front of a small building which he knew to be the barber shop. Bolt chuckled again. Tom had only a couple more buildings to cover. Bolt decided he had timed it just right.

Bolt saw the man walk up behind Tom, but didn't think much of it. The man didn't appear to be sneaking up on Tom or to be any threat. Bolt figured it was someone who was going into the barber shop for a shave. He was too far away to see who it was.

Riding closer, Bolt starred in dumb horror as he realized what was happening. A glint of sunlight bounced off something shiny in the man's hand, struck Bolt's eyes. The man had a gun in his hand. He was moving in on Tom, coming up from behind. Tom didn't know it. Bolt touched his spurs to Nick's flanks, tried to get to Tom to warn him, felt helpless as things happened so fast, it was one big blur.

Bolt saw Tom react at the last minute. He saw Tom swing the hammer backwards. The man jumped back, brought the pistol up, aimed it at Tom. Bolt called Tom's name just as the pistol went off, knew he was too late. Tom fell to the ground as the man ran away. Bolt didn't know if his friend was hit. He saw him crawl over behind a barrel.

It seemed like minutes, but it took Bolt only seconds to reach Tom.

"Are you hit, Tom?" Bolt called as he slid down off his horse in front of the barber shop.

"No. He missed me. Jeez, I didn't even see him coming."

"Who was it?"

"I didn't see him. He got away before I could get a look at him. All I saw was his feet running that way." Tom pointed beyond the building.

"I saw him disappear between those two buildings but I didn't get a good look either. I'll get the bastard, though."

"I'll go with you," Tom said as he jumped up.

"You go around that next building, come up from behind. I'll go between the buildings." Bolt whipped his pistol out, checked it. He stepped over to the narrow passageway between the barber shop and the next building. He ducked his head around the corner of the building, drew it back. It was enough of a glimpse to tell him there was nobody there.

He stepped around the corner into the narrow aisle, checked above him, then kept his eyes trained on the back corners of the buildings. He moved fast, making no sound with his cautious footsteps. Just before he got to the back corner of the building, he heard a noise beyond. He had no way of telling if it was Tom or the bushwacker.

He stuck his head around the corner, glanced to his left. He saw Tom just rounding the corner of the second building over. A rustling noise to his right startled him. He ducked his head back, cocked his hammer. From where he was standing, he spotted the outhouse in the alley. If he could make it across the alley to the cover of the outhouse, he'd have a better chance than being trapped in the long passageway.

He moved out into the alley just far enough to motion for Tom to stay where he was, to stay low. He heard the noise on his right again, ducked back into the passageway.

He took a deep breath, judged the distance to the outhouse. He bent over, made a dash for it.

A shot rang out, the bullet zinged by him, just over his head. He reached the outhouse, took cover behind it. He looked around the edge of it, saw the long water trough behind the barber shop. He heard the noise again, as if someone were moving. This time he was able to pinpoint the sound. It came from behind the water trough.

Just before he ducked back behind the outhouse again, he saw the head pop up from behind the trough. He recognized the face of Dave Talbot. Talbot's head popped back down when he saw Bolt.

Bolt waited, counted to three. Then he peeked around the corner again. He brought his pistol up slowly.

"Come on out of there, Talbot," he taunted. "The game's over."

Talbot raised up quickly, shot at Bolt. Bolt was surprised to see him shooting with his left hand, remembered that his other was broken.

Bolt ducked behind the tiny building just in time. The bullet thudded into the corner of the outhouse, splintered the wood.

Bolt stepped out quickly, caught Talbot half-standing behind the trough. He shot from the hip.

Talbot's eyes went wide with horror as the bullet caught him in the chest. His shirt front exploded with a blossom of bright red blood. His hands shot up in the air, then clutched at his mangled chest. Blood quickly soaked into the gauze bandage around his wounded hand.

Talbot staggered back two feet, tried to keep his balance. He took two steps forward, then toppled over head first into the water trough, his body draped over the edge of the trough. The water reddened around his head and chest which were completely submerged.

Bolt froze when he heard the loud thumping noise beside him. He thought for a moment there had been more than one man after them. He turned his head quickly, whipped his Colt around to face the noise.

The door to the outhouse popped open and a neatly dressed man ran out, his pants down to his knees. He gripped the pants with both hands, tried to pull them up.

"Jeeezus! What's going on?" He looked at Bolt. His face paled when he saw Bolt's pistol aimed at him. "Don't shoot, mister!"

Bolt holstered his pistol.

"Go on back and finish whatever you were doing," Bolt smiled. "The fighting is over."

"I'm done," the gentleman said in a shaky voice. "I wouldn't go back in there if you paid me."

Tom walked up just then. He still had his weapon in his hand.

When the frightened man saw Tom and the pistol, he threw his hands in the air and screamed. He quickly grabbed his pants again, ran away as fast as his tiny

106

steps would allow him, his bare ass bouncing in the breeze.

"You scared the shit out of him," Tom laughed.

"I think I did, poor fellow."

"He'll have something to tell his grandkids someday."

"I'll bet it'll be a cold day in hell before he'll ever set foot in another outhouse."

"That was damned good shooting, Bolt. I thought you were a goner when you ran out in the open like that. Did you see who you killed?"

"One guess."

"Rader?"

"Close. It was Talbot." Bolt walked over to the water trough, Tom right behind him. Bolt reached into the reddened water, grabbed a clump of hair. He pulled Talbot's head out of the water, looked at it, then let it drop back down.

"I'll be damned," said Tom. "How could he shoot with his hand bandaged like that."

"Used the other hand."

"Whew," Tom whistled. "That must have taken a lot of practice to switch hands like that so quick."

"I'm sure it did." Bolt shook his head.

"And all in vain."

"Yep. That's the way life goes sometimes. Tom, will you stop at the undertaker's and tell him he's got a customer? I'm going back to the hotel and make some notes for the meeting." He took his pocket watch out, checked the time. "It's ten-thirty. I'll work on the notes for a while and when you get back, we'll go eat lunch. And then it'll be about time to head over to the meeting. I sure hope we get a good turnout."

"Hard Luck Hal and his bunch will be there. The other miners, too, I think. But do you think you should go through with it now that Talbot's dead?"

"The fact that he came gunning for you is all the more reason to hold this meeting."

"Rader's gonna come down hard on us, ain't he?"

"It wouldn't surprise me. I don't think Rader will show up at the meeting, but keep your eyes peeled. Anything could happen."

"And probably will," Tom added.

Chapter Eleven

Calvin Rader heard the distant shot just as he opened the door to leave the sheriff's office.

"Was that a gunshot?" asked Pete Booker who was right behind him.

"Sounded like it. Probably them miners drinking and fighting over their pokes again."

"This time of day?"

"Who knows? At least it doesn't concern us. We're here and Talbot's still sick."

"I thought he'd be at work today."

"That hand is giving him a lot of pain. He was in tough shape when I was out there yesterday morning. I told him to take a couple days off." Rader didn't tell Booker, but he was a little ticked that Talbot hadn't come in this morning. He was beginning to worry about the gunman Talbot hired, whether he'd show this afternoon like Talbot promised. Rader decided he'd ride out to Talbot's and check it out if Talbot didn't come to work by noon.

Rader spotted the flier just then, the one that was

tacked to the post near the sheriff's door. He glanced at it. His mouth fell open when he read a few key words. He leaned over, read it more carefully.

"What the hell . . . ? Look at this, Pete."

"What's that?" Booker looked over Rader's shoulder, read the print on the flier.

"Looks like Bolt's pulling some funny business."

"Bolt's calling a public meeting at the town hall? I don't believe it."

"Who in hell does he think he is?" Rader snorted, his thin lip curling to a snarl. "First he butts into our business, then he sleeps with our schoolmarm. And now this. I guess he wants to run the whole damned town."

"Are you going to try and stop him?"

"From running the town?"

"No. From having this meeting."

"Hell, no," Rader laughed. "Nobody'll show up. The people in this town are too smart to be hoodwinked by that fuckin' outlaw."

Suddenly, Booker held his hand in the air, cocked his head.

"Listen," he said. "Was that another gunshot. Maybe some fool is shooting lizards just for the hell of it. Let's get back to the store."

"The two men turned and walked toward Rader's store which was two buildings away.

"Look at all them posters," Pete said.

"Hell, they're every damned place you look."

"Looks like Bolt's serious."

"Yeah, well he's wastin' his time."

Both men heard the twin shots that were fired in rapid succession.

110

"I don't like it," Pete said. "Something's going on. I can feel it. Even the town's quiet for this time of morning. Hardly any people on the streets."

"You ain't gettin' spooked, are you, Pete?" Rader kidded as they reached the store. "Well, I'll be damned. Look at that. Bolt had the fuckin' nerve to put a poster on my door. How dare him." Rader snatched the flier off the door, tore it into tiny pieces and threw it to the ground. His face flushed with renewed anger. He opened the door to his shop, shouted at the young boy who worked for him.

"Tommy! Get out here!"

"What's the matter, Mister Rader?" Tommy asked when he got to the front of the store.

"How come you allowed Bolt to put that poster on my door?"

"What poster?" Tommy said, looking the door over.

"That one." Rader pointed to the scraps of poster on the ground then made a sweeping gesture with his gloved hand, indicating the other posters that were visible from there. "Just like all the rest of them."

Tommy, a freckled-faced boy, looked around, scratched his head.

"I didn't allow Bolt to do anything. He never asked. I never even seed him."

"The poster was there. Right there." Rader jabbed a finger at the small tack that remained on the door, the shreds of white paper around it.

"I didn't know nothin' about it," Tommy said, shrugging his shoulders. "I was minding the store, like you said to."

"Forget it," Rader said. "Not your fault."

They all went inside and five minutes later, Rader

walked outside. He was getting edgy because Dave Talbot hadn't shown up. He had told Dave to take one day off, not two like he had told Booker. Dave could have sent his Chinese housegirl, Lin Wing, into town with a message if he planned to take another day off. Of all days, he needed Dave more than others. He couldn't even tell Pete Booker he was worried. Booker was easy-going, not a trigger-happy fellow like Talbot. Booker wouldn't understand about the hired gunman coming to town. It was a secret that only he and Talbot shared.

The pressure was getting to him, he knew. Things were moving too damned slow to suit him and his patience was running thin. Madge had given him her ultimatum and he knew she meant to stick to it. He either had to get rid of Bolt and close the bordello, or she'd leave him. He didn't know what he'd do if she left him. It wasn't only her money, but he still loved her, despite her bitchiness lately.

He looked up when he heard someone running along the wooden boardwalk. He recognized the tow-headed boy who was running toward him. Young Barry Fisher almost knocked into him as he sped by, his head lowered, his arms swinging.

"What's the hurry, Barry?" Rader called.

"Dave Talbot's been shot and I got to tell the sheriff."

"Talbot?" Rader grabbed the boy's arm, whirled him around. "Wait a minute. Did you say Dave Talbot?"

"Yes, sir. He's dead. I gotta get the sheriff quick." He tried to tear his arm lose from Rader's clutches, but Rader held tight.

"Are you sure?" Rader's face paled with the shocking news.

"Yes, sir. I seen him dead back there behind the barber shop. His head was floatin' in the water trough. It was awful. The water was all red. I almost threw up."

"What were you doing behind the barber shop?"

"I was just gonna use the outhouse back there, but when I saw him like that . . ."

"Who killed him?" Rader pressed.

"I don't know. The only person I saw was old man Wales and he wasn't even back there. He was runnin' down the street with his pants at half mast like he was scared or something. I saw him first and didn't think nothin' about it. Figured there'd been a snake in the outhouse. I don't think he killed Talbot, do you?"

"No."

"I'm real sorry about your friend, Mister Rader, but I've gotta go tell the sheriff."

Rader released his grip on the boy's arm. He started trembling when the boy left. It couldn't be true. Dave just couldn't be dead. Desperate, Rader opened the door to his store, stuck his head inside.

"Pete! Come here. Quick!"

"Yeah?" Pete said when he got to the door. "What's the matter, Calvin? You look sick as a dog."

"Talbot's dead."

"What? No, I don't believe it."

"Those shots we heard. That was Talbot cashing in. Behind Ackroyd's barber shop. That's where them shots came from." His words came in short, halting phrases as he struggled to keep his emotions in check.

"Who did it?"

"I'll bet money it was Bolt. Come on, let's get over there," Rader said as he took off on a dead run.

The undertaker was already there by the time Rader

and Booker reached the scene of the fatal shooting. He had pulled Talbot's head out of the water, stretched him out on the ground.

Rader took one look at Talbot's body, the hole in his chest, and got sick to his stomach.

"Any clues who killed him?" Rader asked the thin, balding undertaker, Ross Burtram.

"Don't need clues," Burtram said as he dragged the body closer to his buckboard. "I already know who did it."

"Who?"

"That new fellow in town. Jared Bolt."

"I knew it. Didn't I tell you, Pete?" Rader turned back to the undertaker, a puzzled look on his face. "How'd you find out so quick?"

"Bolt's friend, Mister Penrod, came and told me to pick up the body. Said Bolt killed Talbot in self-defense."

"How the hell could it be self-defense?" Rader protested. "Talbot's shooting hand was busted. Look at it. It's completely bandaged. No way he could have shot at Bolt."

"I can't say about that, but that's how it looks to me. Talbot's pistol was right down there on the ground, right beside him, and it was missing three bullets if he kept it full loaded. It ain't my place to say who's guilty. It's up to the sheriff to decide if it was self-defense or not. I only bury the body."

"The sheriff will be forced to arrest Bolt now," Rader said. "Come on, Pete, let's go."

"Mister Rader, before you go. Who is going to pay for the burial? Did Mister Talbot have any kin?"

"Get your money from Bolt. He's the one who killed him."

Rader got nowhere with Sheriff Pettibone except a promise that he would look into the death of Dave Talbot as soon as possible. Pettibone said he would have a lot of checking to do. He'd have to talk to people who had seen him between the time his hand got busted and the time of his death. When Rader explained that Talbot had stayed out at his farm house and only Lin Wing had seen him, the sheriff said he would have to ride out to talk to her, see if Talbot had been doing any target practicing the past day or two.

Rader was so angry over Pettibone's slowness, he almost forgot about Alexis Townsend. When he remembered, he tried to track her down.

She had already left the schoolhouse by the time he rode over there and he finally found her coming out of the Open Cafe a little before two o'clock that afternoon.

"Miss Townsend, I'd like a word with you."

"Oh, Mister Rader. I didn't see you."

"I'm sorry to have to be the one to tell you this, but the Merchants Association met this morning and voted to fire you. You're through as the schoolmarm as of today."

Her eyes widened in surprise.

"What? I don't understand. For what reason am I being dismissed, if I may ask."

"I think you know the answer to that without asking." Rader clamped his thin lips into a lewd smile, let his eyes fall to her breasts and below.

"No, I don't know. Tell me, please. What are the charges against me?" Her words were cold and bitter.

"You were sleeping with Bolt," he accused. "I'm sure you can understand that that kind of behavior is totally unacceptable to the decent people of this town."

"No, I don't understand that. What I do with my personal life is my own business."

"Not when you are teaching the young, innocent children of this town. As their teacher, you are obligated to teach them right from wrong. You haven't done that, Miss Townsend. You are expected to set a high moral example and we simply cannot tolerate your immoral actions."

"What I do in my own home has nothing to do with the children or morals or anything else."

"I'm sorry, Miss Townsend, but the Merchants Association has voted on the issue and their decision is final."

"Who are they to dictate what I do? A dozen hypocritical men just like yourself. They have no authority to fire me. I'll fight you every step of the way, Mister Rader."

"It won't do any good, lady. So far, the members of the Association are the only ones who know about your immoral actions. If you cause any trouble at all, you can be sure everybody in town will know about your lustful ways."

"That's blackmail, Mister Rader, and you know it."

"Call it what you wish, but those are the facts."

Alexis threw her head back proudly.

"If you'll excuse me now, I'm in a hurry."

"You wouldn't happen to be going to that meeting

your boyfriend has cooked up, would you?"

"That's exactly where I'm going."

"I don't think so." Rader stepped forward, blocked her way.

"You can't stop me from going to a public meeting," she said, trying to get around him.

"Bolt's an outlaw, lady, and for your own good, you'd better stay away from him."

"He is not an outlaw. He's a good man. Better than you."

"He's wanted for murder, lady."

"I heard about Dave Talbot and I know Bolt wouldn't have killed him unless he had a damned good reason. Unless he was defending his own life. I'm positive it was self-defense. Besides, Talbot almost shot Tom Penrod in the back night before last. If Talbot hadn't been so drunk, he might have done it. That man was plumb crazy."

"I wasn't talking about Dave Talbot, lady. Bolt is a wanted man. An outlaw. He is wanted for murdering two lawmen. Why do you think he's on the run?"

"I don't believe you. And stop calling me 'lady.'"

"I guess that term don't fit you anymore, does it? If you don't believe me, go ask Luke Pettibone. He'll set you straight."

"Well I don't believe you. Now if you'll excuse me."

Rader grabbed her arm, dug his fingers into her flesh.

"I wouldn't go to that meeting if I were you. There's likely to be bloodshed if Bolt resists arrest."

"What are you talking about?" She jerked her arm away from his grip.

"The sheriff will be there to arrest Bolt. On two

counts of murder. And since your boyfriend is so trigger-happy, likely there'll be a shootout. Somebody's liable to get killed."

Frightened and on the verge of tears, Alexis turned and walked away as quickly as her trembling legs would take her.

She didn't care about her own problems right then. She had to get over to the town hall to warn Bolt. Rader had detained her so long, she knew she barely had time to make it on time.

She glanced back over her shoulder and when she saw that Rader was walking the other way, she started running. She didn't stop until she got to the town hall.

Her heart sank when she opened the door and went inside. The meeting had already started. She looked around, didn't see the sheriff. She took a seat at the back of the room.

She would have to wait until later to warn Bolt that he was about to be arrested.

Chapter Twelve

Bolt was surprised by the turnout at the meeting he had called. He stood at the front of the large room in the town hall, looked over the group that had assembled. Tom Penrod sat in a chair near the wall, over to Bolt's right. Tom sat facing the audience, watching for trouble. Bolt had not expected the meeting to go without a hitch.

The miners had come in a large group and sat in the front rows. Other townspeople, including some finely dressed women, sat on the middle benches and near the back of the room.

Lucy Tucker and her six prostitutes had braved the occasion and sat on benches behind the bearded miners. The girls wore new tailored street dresses while the miners had not changed from their dusty coveralls.

Bolt scanned the room again with his pale blue eyes, searched for Alexis in the sea of faces. He was disappointed that she was not there. She was the one who had suggested the meeting and since she believed in the same principles that he did, her presence would have given him moral support, if nothing else.

Waiting for her to show up, Bolt stalled as long as he dared. When the crowd became restless at five after two, he had to start without her.

"Ladies and gentlemen," he began, "I don't know if you came here to listen to what I have to say about decency or whether you're here out of curiosity, but I'm glad you're here. If you don't agree with something I say, speak up. If you do agree, tell me so. If you feel like booing me, go ahead and boo. If you want to throw a ripe tomato in my face, then be my guest. Only one thing I ask. No rotten eggs, please. I can't stand the smell."

The miners laughed. Bolt heard a few chuckles from the people in the middle rows, but most of the other people were very reserved.

"What I'm saying is that you people here have the freedom of choice."

The door at the back of the room opened, spilling a shaft of bright sunlight across the middle aisle. Bolt looked up, saw Alexis enter the room and quietly take a seat at the back. He took a deep breath, relaxed, then spoke again, feeling better because she was there.

"I'm a stranger here in town and maybe some of you don't think I have the right to speak up, but when I saw that your freedom was being taken away from you by the members of the Merchants Association, I had to call this meeting."

Bolt heard a few mumbles from the crowd.

"Some of you don't feel that you are giving up your freedom to them, do you?"

The response was divided.

"As you all know, the Merchants Association is

trying to close down Lucy's Place because they want to clean up the town. But closing the bordello will not make this a decent town. If you allow them to close Lucy's there will be more crime here, more killings. Men will leave the town and go elsewhere. The girls, prostitutes, if you will, serve a purpose in society. They can make this a decent town by keeping the men who choose to go there happy.

"If some of you men out there don't want to go to Lucy's Place, then that is your privilege. Nobody condemns you because of your preferences. But don't condemn the ones who want to go there. They have the right to their own preferences. As it stands now, every man in this town has the freedom to decide whether to go to the bordello or not. If you let the dozen members of the Merchants Association make that decision for you, then you are giving up a part of your freedom. If they close the bordello, you will no longer have a choice."

Bolt paused, let his words soak in.

"Do you want a decent town to live in?"

"Yes," came the unanimous response.

"What does decent mean then? Respectable? Good? We all have our own ideas about what is decent and what isn't. To me decency means proper behavior at the proper time. Proper conduct. Proper speech. Proper dress for the proper occasion. Wouldn't you all say that's what decency is about?"

The crowd agreed.

"Let me give you an example," Bolt continued. "That lady near the back. The one in the blue dress. Would you stand up for a minute?"

The lady looked around to make sure Bolt was

pointing at her. With some gentle nudging from the man with her, she finally stood up. Everyone turned to look at her.

"Now wouldn't you say this lady is dressed properly for an afternoon meeting?"

"Yes," they all agreed.

"Then that makes her a decent person. But if she were wearing a nightgown right now, how many of you would think she was decent?"

The miners hooted. Others chuckled.

"On the other hand, if she wore that dress to bed, her husband might not like it."

Everyone laughed. Embarrassed, the woman sat down.

"Now, look at these six girls up here in the fourth row. The girls from Lucy's Place. They are dressed just as properly for an afternoon meeting as that lady in the back. Doesn't that make them decent, too?"

Other than the miners, only a few responded. Bolt wasn't discouraged.

"These prostitutes are decent women. As long as they behave in a proper manner in public, they have every right to be a part of this society. If they don't behave properly, you have every right to see that they are abolished from society. But you have the right to decide that for yourself. Calvin Rader and his bunch are trying to kick these girls out of town and close down the bordello. By doing that, they are taking away your rights to make your own decisions."

Some of those in the audience mumbled among each other.

"That tells me two things about Rader and the members of the Merchants Association," Bolt said.

"First, they think they are smart enough to make all of your decisions for you, and second, they think you are too dumb to make them yourselves. I say keep the bordello open and make your own decisions."

Applause rippled through the crowd and Bolt knew he had them. He talked for another fifteen minutes and then invited their questions.

One man in the back stood up and looked at Bolt with cold eyes.

"You killed Dave Talbot this morning," the man accused. "Do you call that a decent thing to do?"

The question caught Bolt off guard.

"It might not have been a decent thing to do, but it was certainly proper, considering the fact that Talbot provoked the attack and that he was trying to kill me."

Mort Snyder, a neatly dressed man in his forties, stood up.

"I think you're all wrong, Mister Bolt. I'd never go near that bordello and I don't see any need for it. Myself, I think the whorehouse is a blight to this town. I find it offensive."

"What do you find offensive about it?"

"Everything."

"Be more specific. If you've never been inside the bordello, then you must be judging it from outside appearances. Do you find the house itself ugly or offensive?"

"No. It looks like an ordinary house. Nobody would know it was a damned whorehouse unless they lived here."

"Is it the sign out front? The location of the house? I'm trying to find out what you don't like about it."

"It's just knowing that it's there that grates against

123

my sensibilities."

"Then that's something inside you and you're entitled to your opinion. You have the right to decide whether or not you want to visit the bordello. But if it's closed, you will be denying all the other men in this town that same right to make their own decisions."

The man next to Mort Snyder raised his hand, then stood up.

"I disagree with you, Mort," said Hank Cherry. "I wouldn't go to the whorehouse either, but I don't see what that has to do with any of the other fellows around here. Let 'em have it. Hell, as Bolt said, you got a choice. I don't even have a choice. My wife makes those decisions for me."

The women in the group giggled.

"Let the bordello stay," Cherry continued. "It can't hurt us. In fact, since there aren't enough women to go around in this town, let the harlots take care of the overflow. At least it will keep the horny men happy so they don't go around messing with our wives."

"Good point," said Bolt. The discussion went on for another fifteen minutes. Bolt knew the townspeople were still divided, but at least they had listened to him.

"I know some of you don't go along with what I'm saying, but at least you got a chance to express your opinions. That's more than you got from Rader and his bunch." He thanked them for coming, promised them he'd help make Angel's Camp a better place to live.

Alexis waited at the back of the room while the townspeople filed out. She went up to the front as the miners were shaking Bolt's hand, talking to Tom.

"I've got to talk to you, Bolt," she said.

Bolt turned, saw the urgency in her eyes.

"I'll be right with you," he said, shaking Dinger's hand.

"It's important."

Hard Luck Hal stepped up to Bolt, slapped him on the back.

"You did good, Bolt," he said with a toothless grin. "Let me buy you boys a drink."

"Later," Bolt said.

"You got a deal. We'll be over to the Dry Creek Saloon come evenin'. See you then, partner."

As the miners were leaving, Bolt turned to Alexis, saw the paleness of her face.

"Something happened to you, didn't it?" he said.

"I've been fired, but that's not what I want to tell you."

"What do you mean you've been fired?"

"Rader told me just before the meeting. That's why I was late." She quickly told him what Rader had said about them sleeping together and about the Association voting to dismiss her.

Bolt's expression hardened.

"They can't fire you, Alexis. They don't have any say so in the matter. They have no authority at all."

"Listen to me, Bolt. You're in danger. The sheriff was supposed to be here to arrest you during the meeting. For murder."

"I figured they'd get around to that when Rader found out about Talbot."

"It isn't Talbot's death. Rader said you were wanted for killing two lawmen."

"Hell," said Tom, "I thought they'd give up on them charges a long time ago."

"So did I," said Bolt.

"Then it's true?" Alexis said quietly. "You really did kill two lawmen?"

"Phony charges," Tom said. "Bolt had only two choices. Kill them both or be killed himself."

"I knew it was something like that," Alexis sighed. "But you've got to be careful, Bolt. You've got to hide out. If the sheriff arrests you, you'll go to jail. You'll have to prove you're innocent and in this town that won't be easy."

"I don't hide out and I don't run away from things like that, Alexis. If the sheriff arrests me, I'll worry about that when the time comes. Now, about your job. The Merchants Association can't fire you, so don't worry about it. You're a good teacher and the town needs you."

"But Rader said . . ."

"I don't give a damn what he said. You're the teacher here and if Rader gives you any trouble about it, he'll have to answer to me."

Alexis threw herself into Bolt's arms.

"Oh, Bolt. I'm so afraid. I'm afraid for all of us."

Bolt held her tight. He was scared too. Damned scared. If he was arrested and put in jail, he'd never get the chance to prove his innocence. Rader would use his power to keep him there until he rotted in some stinking cell.

Rader had reasons for wanting him out of the way, Bolt knew. The bastard also had enough money to bribe the sheriff.

Bolt thought about Rader's wealthy wife, Madge, wondered where she got her money. Nobody had ever mentioned it. Nobody seemed to know.

He thought about the Madge he had known back in

Tombstone. The beautiful Madge Garrett with her beautiful red hair, her bright green eyes. He had wanted her so much back then. But when she offered herself to him, he had turned her down. It was one of those times in life that he had lived to regret.

Something clicked in Bolt's mind when he remembered Madge Garrett way back then.

And then he knew who Calvin Rader was married to.

Madge Garrett always did have a way with money. She saved every cent she earned, invested it wisely and doubled her profits. She had told Bolt, way back then, that someday she would have enough money to live like a queen.

He had never doubted her.

Chapter Thirteen

Rader stood at the front window of his Mercantile Store, peering over the sign in the window. His stomach churned as he watched the people of the town streaming back from the meeting at the town hall. He was stunned by the number of the throng. He hadn't thought Bolt stood a chance in hell of getting more than a handful of miners to show up for that damned meeting.

He stroked his thin moustache, studied the faces of the people who walked by, trying to determine what they were thinking.

Among the men out there were some of the most uprighteous citizens of Angel's Camp and he wondered if they had been swayed by Bolt's words. That could only mean trouble for him. If he didn't get that bordello closed down soon, Madge was going to leave him. He was running out of time and he didn't think the sheriff was ever going to get around to arresting Bolt.

While Bolt's meeting was in progress, Rader had paid another visit to the sheriff, demanding that he nab

Bolt during the meeting. Luke Pettibone had stalled him again, stating that he still didn't have enough proof to warrant an arrest. Pettibone had also informed him that Dave Talbot's death was a closed issue.

"Absolutely a case of self-defense on Mister Bolt's part," Luke had told him. "I checked with Talbot's Chinese housegirl and she told me that Dave Talbot had spent the entire day, the day before, target shooting with his left hand. He practiced long enough to be able to hit his mark nine out of ten times."

Rader had threatened the sheriff with his job again, but Pettibone had promised only to handle things in due course of time. Rader had come away from the sheriff's office discouraged, but now, watching the townspeople, his mood changed to depression.

Mort Snyder entered the store and Rader turned away from the window and walked over to him.

"What can I help you with, Mort?"

"Nothing right now. I just left that special meeting at the town hall and I wanted to tell you about it."

"Oh, you went to that?" Rader laughed nervously, trying to act nonchalant. He picked at the last bit of tar on his thumb, kept his head down. "I'm surprised. I thought you were dead-set against prostitution."

"I am. That's why I wanted to talk to you. You've got to get that bordello closed down before Bolt gets those people to thinking that frolicking at the whorehouse is as moral as attending a church social. Bolt's got a way with words that's pretty convincing. He almost makes you feel like what he's saying is your own idea. He preached about everyone having the choice to make their own decisions and I let him know that my choice was to stamp out prostitution."

"How'd the others react?"

"I think he managed to swing some of them to his way of thinking, but there were a lot of us who told him we were standing firm on the issue."

"Good for you, Mort. Don't worry, we'll get that whorehouse closed down, even if I have to go there myself and set a torch to it. That would drive them harlots out."

"If you need any help, let me know. I can get all the church men to provide a united front. Only thing is, I think some of them are afraid of Bolt's gun."

"I don't think we'll have to worry about Bolt much longer. The sheriff's fixin' to arrest him any time now."

"That's good news. Good luck."

After Mort was gone, Rader went to the rear of the store and told Pete Booker he was going home for the day.

"Aren't you feeling well?" Pete asked.

"No, I'm not feeling well," Rader snapped. The pressure was mounting and he had to get out of there. He hated the thought of going home and listening to his wife whine about his failures, but he had no other place to go. He went out to the corral behind the store, mounted his horse and rode away, leaving one set of problems to face another. As the horse trotted along on the country road, Rader devised several plans to accomplish his goals. He was beginning to think that he'd have to do everything himself. So far, nobody else had done a damned thing for him.

Madge came into the kitchen a couple of minutes after Calvin entered through the back door.

"You're home early," she said. "Are you ill?"

"A lot you care," Calvin said sarcastically. "Can't a

man enter his own home without getting a bunch of bullshit from his wife?"

"I was only concerned . . ."

"Drop it, Madge. I don't need your fucking sympathy. All I need is to be left alone."

Madge tensed at his words, gritted her teeth. Her green eyes glittered with hatred. A hatred born of fear.

"Was Bolt arrested today?" she asked.

"I don't need your nagging. Not now." He opened the cupboard door, took out the jar of ointment and started to rub it into the sores on his hand.

"Well, was he?"

"No. The sheriff is taking his time. He's stalling me for some reason."

"What about the bordello? I assume you got that closed today."

"No, it isn't closed yet. Just leave me alone, Madge!" He threw the jar of ointment at the counter, stormed out of the room and went into his study where he could have some peace.

Madge ran up the stairs in tears. She slammed her bedroom door, sat down at the dressing table and covered her eyes. She was shaking but she didn't know if it was because of Calvin's mood or whether she was frightened to learn that nothing had been done to get rid of Bolt. That was her main concern right then.

While she was sitting there, she decided to make her own move. If Calvin was too weak to be forceful with Luke Pettibone, she'd see the sheriff herself.

She changed her dress quickly, brushed her hair again. She wrapped a thin green scarf around her head to keep her hair in place while she was riding in the carriage. She took her carpetbag from the shelf, opened it

131

to put a clean handkerchief inside. At the bottom of the purse was the small hide-out pistol Calvin insisted she carry ever since Hank Cherry's wife had been raped two months before. She started to take it out to lighten her purse. When she thought of Claudine Cherry, she left the loaded pistol in the bottom of her purse.

Outside, she asked Tony Ringer and Mac Cahn, the two men who worked for them, to prepare the carriage for a trip to town.

It took fifteen minutes to hitch the horses to the carriage and a half hour later, the carriage pulled up in front of the sheriff's office. Tony Ringer looped the reins around the bar in front of him, climbed down from the driver's seat and walked around the carriage to help Missus Rader down. He rolled a cigarette from his makings, leaned against the carriage to wait for her return.

Luke Pettibone stood up when Madge entered his office.

"What can I do for you, Missus Rader?"

"I want to know why you haven't arrested that man named Bolt. I understand that you are aware of the fact that he is a wanted criminal."

"These things take time, Missus Rader."

"Is that the way you run this town, Sheriff? You mean to tell me that a man can go out and commit a crime and you'll sit around and wait until you're good and ready before you go out and arrest him?"

Pettibone leaned back in his chair, picked up his cigar and lit it with a match. He took a puff, tipped his head back and blew the smoke in the air.

"The crime Bolt is wanted for wasn't committed in Angel's Camp. It happened so long ago that I have to be sure it hasn't already been resolved. I'm waiting for some proof now. I told all this to your husband earlier."

"Yes. That's why I'm here. The women in Angel's Camp are outraged that the bordello is still open and we know that Bolt is the cause of it."

"That's not my business, ma'am. My job is to keep the law. There is no law against the operation of a house of prostitution in this town. I suggest that if you want it outlawed, you make a law to that effect. Then I'll close it down. My hands are tied until a law is on the books."

"You don't need a law passed to arrest Bolt," she challenged. "You already know he's wanted by the authorities. Why didn't you arrest him when he was having his meeting this afternoon? Surely you saw the signs. You knew where he was."

Pettibone knocked the ashes from his cigar, cleared his throat. He didn't want to admit that he was afraid of Bolt, afraid of his fast gun. He had purposely stayed away from Bolt's meeting because he figured there'd be trouble. If there had been trouble, he knew he'd have to go settle it. That was his job. The truth of the matter was, he was afraid to arrest Bolt. He cringed every time he thought about it. That was why he had stalled so long.

"I told you, these things take time."

"Well, if you want my opinion, Sheriff Pettibone, your time is about up. The women of this town are afraid to leave their homes since Bolt came to town. If you can't guarantee us a safe, decent place to live, then we'll get a sheriff who can."

"Settle down, Missus Rader. You don't understand

133

the complications of this job."

"I'll tell you what I do understand. You are being paid to protect us and you're not doing your job. We'll see that you're replaced with someone who will."

"Now, Missus Rader . . ."

"No. It's too late for any more excuses. If Bolt isn't arrested by sunset, which is only an hour away, I'll guarantee you the women of this town will picket your office. I'll get all the top society women I can and we'll carry signs in front of this building to let everyone know that you're not doing your job. You'll lose your job unless you arrest Bolt right away."

Pettibone stroked his chin, looked away while he thought. He knew she meant what she said. He didn't like the pressure she was putting on him, but he knew the time had come when he would have to face Bolt.

"I'll tell you what I'm going to do, Missus Rader. I can go ahead and arrest Bolt, hold him here in jail until I get the information I need. If he is, in fact, a fugitive from the law, I will turn him over to the proper authorities. But, understand this, if he is no longer a wanted man, I will have to release him."

"That sounds fair enough." Madge got up, satisfied that Sheriff Pettibone would keep his promise.

After she left, Pettibone decided that he would not face Bolt alone. He would deputize two of the toughest men he knew. Then he would be prepared to search Bolt out. He would be ready to make his arrest.

Madge's knees went weak when she saw him. She had just come out of the sheriff's office, was walking over to her carriage when she glanced down the street.

Her heart skipped a beat. Her skin tingled with a sudden flush when she saw Bolt walking out of the Angels Hotel which was only six buildings on down the street from the sheriff's office.

Bolt was with Tom Penrod and she recognized both of them immediately. There was no mistaking Bolt's tall, muscular body, the way he carried himself as if he owned the world. And Tom, a couple of inches shorter than Bolt, but lean and lanky, his casual stride that made him look like he had not a care in the world. She knew them so well, she could almost see their smiles as they talked to each other, Bolt's pale blue eyes dancing when he smiled.

Turning her head away, she quickly stepped over to the carriage, covered the lower part of her face with her thin green scarf. She was sure that Bolt had not seen her. Tom and Bolt were talking to each other as they came out of the hotel and were not looking her way.

Tony Ringer offered his arm to help her up on the seat of the carriage. Keeping the scarf across her face, she climbed up, scooted across to her side of the carriage. When she looked down the street again, she got only another quick glimpse of Bolt and Tom before the two friends turned into the Dry Creek Saloon next door to the Angels Hotel.

Madge leaned back against the carriage seat, realized how tense she was. She thought about how she had felt when she first learned that Bolt was in Angel's Camp. The initial shock when Calvin had first mentioned his name. That shock turning to fear. The fear gradually eating at her until it turned in to panic when she realized how Bolt's appearance in Angel's Camp could destroy her happiness, her comfortable way of

135

life, her social status, her relationship with friends. He had the power to turn her whole life around.

The expensive carriage, dusty now from the dirt roads, creaked, moved slowly away from the boardwalk as Ringer snapped the reins over the horse's shoulders. The wooden wheels made a full circle, picked up speed as the carriage passed by the Mercantile Store. When they went by the front of the Dry Creek Saloon, Madge kept her eyes on the batwing doors, hoping for another glimpse of Bolt. After the horse and carriage turned the corner at the end of the street, she lowered the scarf from her face, moved it again to cover her hair from the dust. She felt relief that Bolt had not seen her, but mixed with that relief was a sense of disappointment that her glimpse of Bolt and Tom had been so brief.

She wished she was in the position to go up to them, throw her arms around them and then sit for hours talking about old times. She wanted to know what they had been doing since she last saw them. She wanted them to know that she had a good life now. But she knew it was too late for that now.

Madge finally relaxed as the carriage bounced along the rutted road, tried to sort out the confusion in her mind. She thought about Bolt being arrested and felt guilty. When she thought about what would happen to her life if Bolt discovered that she lived in Angel's Camp, the panic returned.

She was desperate, but could she live with her conscience if Bolt was arrested, jailed, or possibly executed because she had pressured the sheriff to arrest him? She knew he wasn't guilty of those murder charges so long ago. Yes, Bolt had killed the two brothers who were lawmen, but only in self-defense.

She didn't really want Bolt arrested, or hurt or killed. She just wanted him to leave town without ever knowing she was there.

The carriage turned off the main dirt road onto a smaller one. She realized that they were almost home and she still didn't know what to do. When she saw her own elegant, rambling home come into view, Madge told the driver to turn the carriage around and head back to town. He gave her a puzzled look, shrugged his shoulders.

She didn't know what she was going to do there, but she knew she had to see what happened to Bolt.

Madge had already done what she had to do.

The fates would take care of everything else.

Chapter Fourteen

From the Rader home, the trip back to town was a good half hour's ride in a horse-drawn carriage. By horseback, a little less. By the time Madge returned to town, more than an hour had passed since she had first seen Bolt and Tom coming out of the Angels Hotel and entering the saloon next door.

"Where do you want to go?" Tony Ringer asked as he guided the carriage around the corner and back onto the main street of town. "Back to the sheriff's office?"

"No," Madge said. "Just pull up in front of the Open Cafe."

Ringer eased the reins to the right. The horse responded, moved to the edge of the street. When they were in front of the cafe, Ringer reined back and the carriage creaked to a stop.

Two doors away from the Open Cafe was the Angel's Camp Freight and Stage Depot building which also housed the telegraph office. Hank Cherry's Freight & Shipping Company occupied the warehouse which had been built onto the back of the stage depot building.

Directly across the street from the stage depot were the Dry Creek Saloon and the Angels Hotel. The Mercantile Store and the sheriff's office were on the same side of the street as the saloon and hotel, but several buildings to the left from as Madge faced that side of the street.

Sitting in the carriage, Madge faced the stage depot and the saloon across the street. By turning in the seat, she also had a good view of the Mercantile Store and the nearby sheriff's office.

The small town was busy that time of evening. It was after six o'clock and already the street was taking on the gray casts of shadows that came just before dusk. The people who bustled about on the boardwalks, walked with a purpose instead of a casual stroll. Men who were just finishing a long day's work headed for one of the restaurants or to a cozy home where supper was waiting. For those who worked in the fields, such as the miners, the ranchers, the farmers, it was the time of day to come in to town instead of leaving it.

Not knowing what to do or where to go now that she was back in town, Madge remained in the carriage. She watched men come and go through the batwing doors of the Dry Creek Saloon, wondered if Bolt was still inside. Maybe he was back in his hotel room, safe from harm. Maybe he and Tom had gone to the bordello where Tom would enjoy the services offered by the girls. If he hadn't changed in the past few years, Bolt would spend his time at the bordello talking to the madam, joking with the girls or playing poker with anyone who would join him. But Bolt would not pay for the services of one of the girls.

Madge wondered if Bolt had been arrested in the

hour she had been gone. She glanced back at the sheriff's office, pictured Bolt locked up in some god-awful cell. She wondered if it was all just a big bad dream that would go away when she woke up.

"Are you going inside?" Tony Ringer asked.

"What?" she said, startled by his voice. She was so wrapped up in her own thoughts, she had forgotten that she was not alone.

"Are you going inside the cafe to eat or do you want me to go in and get something for you?"

"Oh, no thanks. I'm not hungry."

Ringer gave her a puzzled look, shook his head. He climbed down from the carriage seat to stretch his legs. He dug the makings out of his pocket, built a cigarette, decided he would never understand the way a woman thought.

Madge watched the batwing doors of the saloon, debated whether to risk going over there and peeking inside to see if Bolt was still there. But she could not force herself to leave the security of her carriage.

The stage coach, when it arrived, kicked up dust and dirt as it rolled by Madge's carriage at a good clip. The stage pulled in ahead of her, jerked to a halt in front of the stage depot, a few buildings beyond the Open Cafe. Madge turned her head away from the street, shielded her eyes and face from flying grit, looked around again when the dust settled.

Madge watched the driver jump down from the seat, flex stiff muscles. She watched the passengers begin to disembark. Madge was grateful for the diversion the stage arrival provided. It took her mind off her worries and it made her seem less of a fool for just sitting in her carriage.

"You waiting for one of them stage passengers?" Tony Ringer called up to her from where he stood near the carriage.

"No, I'm not expecting anyone," she said.

Ringer flicked the cigarette butt to the ground, kicked idly at the dirt with the toe of his boot. The Raders paid him well for working for them and he did what he was told. But this was the damnedest thing he'd ever seen. He had tried to figure out why Madge Rader sat in the carriage like a beautiful statue but he gave up. He was beginning to think that she had lost her mind.

The stage coach driver, who was a balding, barrel-chested man, jumped down from the hard wooden seat, flexed the muscles that were beginning to stiffen from the long haul over bumpy dirt roads. He walked back, opened the passenger door of the stage, then took a white envelope out of his shirt pocket, walked over to the stage depot door and went inside.

After the clerk greeted him by name, the stage driver handed the envelope to the clerk.

"There's more mail out in the stage, but this is an important letter for Alexis Townsend. I was told that it had to be delivered to her as soon as I got here."

"I'll take care of it," said the stage depot clerk. "I'll deliver it myself on my way home. After I check the mail bag in, I'm ready to close up, call it a day."

"I know what you mean."

"How many passengers do you have?"

"Four. Two of them get off here. The other two will be riding on with me in the morning. Any new passengers for the morning departure?"

"Not so far. Check with me in the morning when you're ready to leave. Have a nice evening."

"I will. Same to you."

The stage driver went back outside, unloaded the luggage for three of his passengers. The fourth passenger didn't have luggage.

Hardy Bragg was the last passenger to leave the stage. He didn't need any luggage, hadn't brought any. He wouldn't be on the stage when it left in the morning. He wouldn't even be spending the night in Angel's Camp. He would do what he had been paid to do and then pick up the horse Dave Talbot promised him. He'd ride out of town, spend the night out under the stars before heading back to Sacramento.

Bragg was not a big man, but he was powerful, tough as nails. His arms were thick with muscles. He wore faded blue jeans, a plaid shirt and his pistol low on his leg. He had shaggy, unkempt hair, a moustache and dark beady eyes.

Sure that his old friend, Dave Talbot, would be there to greet the stage, Bragg looked around, didn't see him. He dug a plug of tobacco out of his pocket. He leaned against the wall, watched the other passengers pick up their luggage from the boardwalk and head across the street to the hotel. The stage driver carried a bag of mail inside the stage depot, came back out and moved the carriage around to the back where the horses would be taken care of for the night, the stage cleaned before the morning departure.

Bragg chewed his tobacco and waited for Talbot. That was all he could do. Talbot had promised him that Calvin Rader would pay him five hundred bucks and a horse to kill a man named Bolt. He needed Talbot to

142

tell him where Bolt was, what he looked like.

After waiting fifteen minutes, Bragg became impatient, decided to go looking for Talbot. The sun was gone and it would be dark in another fifteen minutes. He spat the wad of tobacco to the ground, turned to go into the stage depot to ask directions to Talbot's home. The door was locked. The stage depot clerk had already locked up for the night, gone out the back door.

Hardy Bragg had already spotted the Dry Creek Saloon. He'd try over there. If Dave Talbot was still drinking as much as he used to, more than likely that's where he'd be. Bragg was ready for a drink himself, after the long dusty trip. He'd have a drink, but only one. He had a man to kill and he made it a fast rule never to have more than one drink when he was a paid assassin. That's why he never failed, why he had the reputation as the best in the West. He never allowed alcohol to interfere with his work like Talbot did.

Bragg sauntered over to the Dry Creek Saloon, pushed through the batwing doors. He stood just inside the doorway for a moment, scanned the smoke-filled room. It was Friday night and the saloon was jammed with noisy customers. The clinking piano notes were barely audible above the din of the bar. Bragg studied each face, didn't see Talbot. Finally, he threaded his way through the tables, the men standing around. He elbowed a position at the long counter where he stood for several minutes before the bartender came up to take his order.

"What'll it be?" said the tall, emaciated bartender.

"Whiskey," Bragg answered.

The bartender poured two three fingers in a small

tumbler, slid it across the counter to Bragg.

"Do you know Dave Talbot?" Bragg asked.

"Yep."

"Know where I might find him?"

"You won't. You missed him by a few hours. He's dead, mister."

Shocked by the news, Bragg took a sip of the whiskey, cursed to himself. He still had a job to do. He had promised Talbot. He knew he would get his money from Rader. Talbot had promised him that.

"Do you know a man they call Bolt?"

"Yep. I know who he is."

"Do you know where he is right now?"

"Sure. Right over there." The bartender nodded his head toward the table in the corner. "Just beyond where them miners is sitting. That's Bolt in the corner with his friend Penrod."

Bragg looked in the direction the barkeep had nodded. He saw the two men at the table.

"Which one is Bolt?"

"You a friend of his?" the bartender said suspiciously.

"Yeah. Long time since I've seen him, though. Thought I'd surprise him."

"Bolt's the one with the dark shirt."

"Thanks." Bragg slapped a coin on the counter, told the bartender to keep the change. He picked up his drink, carried it to the other side of the room where he could get his bearings.

At first he mingled with other men who were standing around drinking so that he would not be so obvious. He studied Bolt, wished he was not at the corner table. It made his job more difficult. He studied the angles, made his decision. He tipped the tumbler up, drank until the whiskey was gone, set the empty glass on a nearby table.

Bragg moved into position without anyone taking notice of him. He stood five feet away from Bolt, his back against the wall. He was just about to draw his pistol when one of the miners walked over to Bolt and set a full drink before him. The miner blocked his vision of Bolt and Bragg cursed.

The miner moved away, sat down at the next table with the other miners.

This time, Bragg eased his pistol out of the low-slung holster. He kept it tight against his leg. He waited. Waited till he was sure nobody was watching him. He waited until Bolt had turned his head the other way.

Keeping it close to his body, Bragg brought the pistol up slowly, eased the hammer back. The click was almost silent in the noisy room. He slipped his finger into the trigger, was about to pull the trigger when he saw the men out of the corner of his eye.

He turned his head, saw the three men approaching Bolt's table. All three of them wore shiny tin badges.

It was almost dark outside when Madge noticed Sheriff Pettibone and his two deputies emerge from the sheriff's office. Her heart quickened as she watched them march toward the Dry Creek Saloon. She reminded herself that things were out of her control now.

She leaned forward in the seat when the sheriff and his men pushed their way through the batwing doors. She tried to remain calm. But she couldn't. She had to see what was happening to Bolt. She had to be there to stop the sheriff if it came to a shootout.

Madge scrambled down from the carriage, ran across the street.

Tony Ringer was dumbfounded. He started to call out to her, said to hell with it.

Madge rushed up to the batwing doors, looked inside. She couldn't see Bolt at all. There were too many men in the way.

She dashed around to the side of the building, looked into a window, found that it was curtained. She ran around back, found the back door unlocked. She opened the door, slipped into a small, darkened back room. A shaft of light coming from the saloon, spilled a pale orange light across a strip of the floor in the middle of the room. It was enough light to allow her to make her way across the room without bumping into anything.

She stood in the shadow of the back room, a few inches away from the doorway where the light wouldn't fall on her dark form. She looked into the next room, saw Sheriff Pettibone first. Then she saw the two deputies move in behind the sheriff. She craned her neck, finally spotted Bolt sitting with Tom at the corner table.

She saw the pistol in the sheriff's hand as he approached Bolt's table. She gasped, clutched at her chest, tried to quiet her pounding heart.

When Hardy Bragg saw the sheriff, the deputies on his heels, he quickly eased his pistol back into the holster. He moved along the wall, away from Bolt's table, faded into the group of men who had turned to watch the sheriff.

Bragg was an outlaw, a wanted man. He knew his face was plastered on wanted posters all over the place. He reckoned there wasn't a sheriff in northern California who hadn't seen his picture. He had no intention of being hustled off to jail so he kept his distance.

Besides, maybe the sheriff would do his job for him.

A hush fell over the room as the drinkers turned to gawk at the sheriff.

Bolt looked up when he saw the sheriff step up to the table. He saw the weapon in the sheriff's hand, the two men behind Pettibone. He moved his hand under the table, slid his hand over to his holster.

"Hold it right there, Bolt. You're under arrest," Pettibone said, his pistol aimed at Bolt's chest. "Show your hands. Put 'em on the table or I blast you right now."

Bolt did as he was told, put both hands flat on the table.

"You, too, Penrod," the sheriff said.

"You gotta have a reason to arrest a man, Sheriff, or didn't they tell you that before they gave you that tin star." Bolt glared at Pettibone, leaned back in his chair.

"Don't get smart with me, Bolt. I'm taking you in. I've got reasons to arrest you. Three reasons, as a matter of fact."

"Care to tell me what they are? I'd hate for you to go to all this trouble if your reasons are wrong."

"You know what they are, but I'll remind you in case it's slipped your mind. You're wanted for two counts of murder, murdering lawmen, I might add, and one

147

count of bank robbery."

"Trumped up charges, Sheriff. Self-defense on all three counts."

"Bank robbery can't be self-defense."

"It was in my case," Bolt grinned.

Pettibone's eyes hardened. Bolt was making a damned fool out of him.

"Stand up, Bolt. Put your pistol on the table. You're coming with me."

Bolt glanced over at Tom. They exchanged knowing looks.

"Anything you say, Sheriff. I know you need this arrest to prove you're a big boy." Bolt stood up with a sudden movement. As he did, his hand shot to his holster. His pistol was cocked and aimed at Pettibone before the sheriff realized what he was doing.

Tom jumped up at the same time, drew his pistol, aimed it at the closest deputy.

"You made a mistake, Sheriff," Bolt taunted. "You're supposed to tell me to move nice and slow."

The bystanders chuckled.

Pettibone hated Bolt for this. He wanted to kill him on the spot. But he knew Bolt's reputation. He knew he'd never stand a chance against Bolt's fast gun.

"The fun and games are over, Bolt. Hand your gun over, butt first."

"You said that right, but you're supposed to say please. Didn't your mama ever teach you any manners?"

The miners at the next table roared with laughter. Others chuckled, Hardy Bragg among them. He loved it when someone made an ass out of a lawman. In the shadows of the next room, Madge Rader covered her

148

mouth with her hands, stifled the urge to giggle.

"Goddamn it, Bolt! Do as you're told or I'll put you away forever, you damned smart aleck bastard."

"You want to try it?" Bolt said, his expression dead serious.

Pettibone stood motionless. His eyes went to Bolt's pistol, to his finger in the trigger hole. He figured his chances.

"Go ahead, Sheriff," shouted one of the miners.

"Try it, Pettibone," taunted another miner. "You got a fifty-fifty chance."

Pettibone still didn't move.

"Appears we got us a standoff, Sheriff," Bolt said.

Pettibone, moving with exaggerated slowness, eased the hammer back down, put his pistol back in his holster. He motioned for his deputies to do the same.

"You win this round, Bolt, but if I ever see your face again, I'll blow you away on the spot. You'd better get your ass out of town because if you stay, you'll have to look over your shoulder every damned minute. I'll get to you when you're least expecting it."

Defeated, Sheriff Pettibone turned and walked away.

Bolt had no doubt he meant what he said.

Chapter Fifteen

Calvin Rader paced the floor for a half hour after Madge stormed out of the house. He didn't know where she had gone. She didn't bother to tell him. Maybe she'd gone to put pressure on the sheriff. He didn't know. She had mentioned it. If so, then he hoped it worked.

On the other hand, maybe she had carried out her threat to leave him. She had been angry enough to do it when they had talked just before she left. That was the thing he feared the most. He couldn't exist without her.

He had checked her room to see if she had taken any of her clothes or other belongings. Except for her carpetbag and the clothes she was wearing, everything else was in order.

The pressure was on to get that damned bordello closed down. It was his only chance of saving face, of gaining Madge's respect. He didn't know why she was so damned insistent about the bordello but she had him over a barrel and he had to move fast. He had an idea and if it worked, Lucy would have to close her place.

The girls would disappear one by one until she wouldn't have any girls left to service the men. Sybil Childs would be the first one to disappear.

Rader called Mac Cahn into his study, explained what he wanted him to do. Mac was perfect for the job. He had only been working for Rader for a week and as far as Rader knew, the boy had never been to the bordello before. Lucy Tucker wouldn't recognize him as one of Rader's men.

Rader and Mac rode to the small cabin in the woods. Rader owned the cabin, used it when he went hunting. It was located close to town but deep enough in the woods to be good hunting territory.

Rader stayed at the cabin, sent Mac to fetch Pete Booker. The hardest part of setting his plan in motion was convincing Booker to go along with it.

"I'm not going to harm any of the girls," Rader told him.

"I don't know, Cal. I don't like it."

"We'll take Sybil Childs, keep her here in the cabin. The rest will get scared and leave the bordello of their own accord. Lucy will have to shut down then."

"Won't Madge wonder where you are if you're gone all night?"

"I'll go back home after you two get the girl. You can stay here all night, can't you, Pete? You owe me one. If it wasn't for me, you'd still be shoveling horse shit for a living."

"I'd be glad to stay here and stand guard," Mac offered.

Rader considered it, decided Mac would be better. Pete was getting too soft lately.

It was dark when Pete and Mac arrived at the

bordello fifteen minutes later. They rode around to the side of the building, tied their horses to a tree. Pete waited outside as planned while Mac entered the bordello by the front door.

Mac glanced around the room, saw the glitter gals who were sitting on the couch. He walked over to the small bar at the other end of the room where Lucy was talking to a couple of miners.

"Good evening," Lucy said, "can I get you a drink?" She was glad to see someone besides the miners come in. Not that she didn't like the miners, but business was slow since Rader had started his campaign. The miners were the only ones who still patronized her bordello.

"Is Sybil working tonight?" Mac asked when Lucy poured him a brandy.

"Yes, she's here. She'll be available in a little while. Maybe one of the other girls . . ."

"I'll wait."

"You new in town? I don't think I've seen you before."

"I've been here a week. I hear the town's trying to shut you down. Too bad."

"I reckon there will always be folks trying to shut down the whorehouses in the West. Some folks don't approve."

Mac waited impatiently, drank his drink. It was ten minutes before Lucy told him that she would go up and send Sybil down."

"No need, ma'am. Just tell me where she is."

"Third door on the right."

Mac paid Lucy the money, went upstairs. When Sybil opened the door in her thin, transparent negligee,

Mac wanted her right then. He knew he had to work fast, get her out of there so they would be long gone before anyone missed her.

Mac could wait. He'd have her all to himself the rest of the night.

Hardy Bragg waited until the sheriff and his deputies had left the saloon.

Bolt was sitting down, had just finished holstering his pistol, when Bragg stepped up to his table.

"Think you're real smart, pokin' fun at the sheriff like that," Bragg challenged. "Well in my book, you're a fuckin' coward. You didn't have the guts to pull the trigger."

Bolt looked up, saw the tough-looking man in front of him. He took note of the fact that the stranger stood with both arms hanging loose at his sides, his hand within easy reach of the low-slung holster. He'd seen plenty of men like that in his time. Men who thought they were tougher than anyone else, thugs who had to prove their manhood.

"What's it to you, stranger?" Bolt said, leveling his cold eyes on the man.

"I think you talk tough to impress these boozers, but you're a chickenshit coward," Bragg said in a loud abrasive voice.

Heads turned in their direction. Men mumbled to each other.

"If you're lookin' for kicks," Bolt said, "why don't you go play with your pud?"

The miners at the next table chuckled.

"I'm gonna kill you, you stinkin' yellow belly," Bragg

threatened, moving his hand above his holster. "Let's see if you have the guts to try and stop me."

Chairs screeched against the hardwood floor as the spectators started moving away from the arguing men. They spread out, gave Bolt and the stranger a wide berth. The men stopped mumbling to each other. The silence was deafening.

Bolt knew he was in a hard spot. Men like that wouldn't stop until they had pushed too far. He had killed desperados before, knew their routine. Jammed into the corner like he was, gave him the disadvantage. He knew this ruffian would risk his life to prove his point.

Moving slowly, Bolt scooted his chair back. The scraping noise echoed in the quiet room. Men gasped, waited for the gunplay to erupt. Bolt stood up, let his arms fall to his side, loose, limber, ready to move.

"You care to step outside and talk about it?" Bolt asked.

"No. I want your friends to see what kind of a fuckin' coward you are."

Bragg's hand moved up, hovered over his pistol.

Bolt brought his hand up slow. It floated inches away from his holster.

"One of us is gonna die," Bragg said.

"Yeah." Bolt watched the outlaw's eyes as the two men stared at each other. He waited for the signal that would tell him when the man was going to make his move. It was always the same. Bolt didn't know why but men who had put down the challenge always did the same thing. It was the eye movement that told him when the challenger was going to draw. That's why Bolt never looked away from the man's eyes.

154

Neither man moved. They stared at each other, their shooting hands poised above their weapons.

The crowd held their breath in unison.

For just a brief instant, Bragg's eyes shifted to Bolt's shooting hand as if he was testing to see if he could make it.

That was the signal Bolt had been waiting for.

Both men drew at once. Both cocked their pistols as they cleared leather. Twin shots pierced the silence, just split seconds apart.

Bolt was faster by a beat of the heart. Bragg's eye movement had made the difference.

Bolt's bullet slammed into the stranger's heart and exploded. Bolt leaned to the side as he fired the quick shot. Bragg's bullet missed the side of Bolt's head by the width of a cigarette paper.

Bragg's eyes widened in horror as he took the bullet. His mouth fell slack. The pistol fell from his slack hand, clattered on the hardwood floor. Bragg staggered forward, bumped against the table. He tumbled over backwards, was dead when he crashed to the floor.

The miners cheered. Other men relaxed taut muscles, began to move back into their places.

The bartender announced drinks for the house then had two men drag the body out back, sent a third for the undertaker. He grabbed a bucket of sawdust from under the counter, carried it over to Bolt's table.

"You were damned lucky," the bartender told Bolt as he scattered the sawdust over the trail of blood on the floor.

"So were you," Bolt grinned.

"How so?"

"With a crazy man like that, you're lucky you didn't get your whole damned saloon shot to pieces. All you've got to worry about is the bullet that's buried in the wood behind my head."

"You're right. You just saved me a bundle of money in repairs. By the way, Bolt, I'm sorry I told that man where you were. I didn't know . . ."

Bolt's eyes widened in surprise, then hardened into slits.

"What're you talking about?"

"That feller came in asking for you a few minutes before Sheriff Pettibone showed up. Said he was an old friend of yours and he wanted to surprise you."

"That he did."

"He asked for Dave Talbot first and when I told him Talbot was dead, he asked if I knew you."

"Thanks," Bolt said. "You couldn't have known."

The bartender went back to the bar, relieved that Bolt didn't cuss him out.

"You were set up," said Tom.

"Yeah. Rader and Talbot. Talbot must have been the contact man so this was arranged before I killed Talbot."

"Maybe Talbot was working on his own. Maybe Talbot wanted revenge."

"Nope. Rader's involved. Two reasons your theory don't work. Talbot had as many grudges against you as he did me and the bartender said he asked for me. He tried to kill you twice, but he never came after me. He knew I would be taken care of. And Rader's the only one with enough money to hire an outside gunny."

"Rader's pretty desperate, ain't he?"

"Yeah. Let's get out of here. I think this place is

jinxed for me tonight. Two close calls in one night is enough for me."

Bolt stood up, was saying goodbye to the miners when he saw Alexis Townsend making her way through the crowded saloon, heading toward him, a purse clutched in her hand. He stepped back over to his table, waited for her.

Eli Dingledorf, the tall, thin miner they called Dinger, got up from the couch at the bordello for the fourth time. He walked across the floor, glanced up at the stairway, pulled his pocket watch out and checked the time. He walked on over to the bar, sat down.

"How long do you think it'll be before Sybil's finished?" he asked Lucy.

"You still waiting your turn, Dinger?" Lucy laughed.

"She been up there with that feller a long time."

"She has at that." For the first time, Lucy felt an unknown fear in the pit of her stomach. It wasn't like Sybil to spend so much time with one man. Now that she thought about it, it seemed odd that a man who had never been to the bordello before would ask for her by name. That happened, though, if a man had been referred to a certain girl by a friend, so maybe she was edgy over everything.

"Reckon I'll just have to wait." Dinger started back to the couch.

"Tell you what I'll do," Lucy said. "I'll go up and check on her."

Lucy went upstairs, stopped beside the room Sybil used for her customers. She leaned closer, listened at the door. She didn't hear any sound at all. No low

157

voices, no sounds of love making. Nothing. Her first thought was that Sybil and the customer had fallen asleep.

She tapped softly on the door at first and when she got no response, she pounded with her fist. Finally, she opened the door and looked inside.

Lucy's scream pierced the air.

Dinger took the steps three at a time, pushed by Lucy who was in the doorway.

"My God, she's gone!" he shouted. He saw the curtains flapping at the open window. The bed had been stripped of its covers. One end of a sheet was tied to the leg of the bed; the other end hung out the window.

Lucy stayed in the doorway, stunned, as others gathered around her, craning their necks to see inside.

Dinger rushed to the window, stared down into the darkness. He reeled in the two sheets and blanket that were knotted together.

"That bastard," said Dinger.

"Oh, that poor girl," Lucy said. "Why is it always Sybil? I hope she's all right."

"No signs of a struggle," Dinger said as he glanced around the room. "No blood. Likely she's not hurt. Not yet anyway."

"I wonder how long she's been gone."

"Could be more than a half hour. It's been that long since that stranger went upstairs. I know. I been watchin' the time."

"Oh, what're we going to do?" Lucy cried. "How will we ever find her if she's been gone that long?"

"I'm gonna go find Bolt," Dinger said. "He'll know what to do."

"Hello, Alexis," Bolt said. "Is something wrong?"

"I got it, Bolt," she said. "The letter came on the afternoon stage just like I said it would."

"Good."

"I found out what Madge Rader's maiden name was and how long she's been married to Calvin. Her maiden name was Madge Garr . . ."

The shot seemed to come from thin air. The explosion shattered against Bolt's eardrums.

Bolt's eyes quickly darted around the room. He saw no sudden movement except the others turning around to look in his direction.

Alexis screamed in the wake of the shot reverberations. The force of the bullet knocked her backwards. She clutched a hand to her left arm, up near the shoulder. Warm, sticky blood spilled from the bullet wound, oozed through her fingers. Things began to spin around in her vision. Darkness folded over her brain like petals of a flower.

Before Bolt could get around the table to reach her, Alexis Townsend collapsed to the floor, unconscious, her dress dragged through the fresh sawdust.

Bolt and Tom reached her at the same time. Bolt took a quick look at the wound under her torn sleeve, opened her eyelids to check the pupils.

"Take care of her," he told Tom. I'll be right back."

Bolt dashed to the window on that side of the room. He jerked back the curtain, saw no hole in the glass. In the dark window, there was only the hazy reflection of the confusion inside the saloon as men moved about to see what had happened.

Running through the saloon, Bolt searched the faces of the men there. He sniffed the air as he moved, checking for the stench of fresh gunpowder that would linger after such a shot.

He ran back over to Tom and Alexis, studied the angle of the shot, judging where it would have come from to hit her in the shoulder. He looked behind him, saw the open door that led to the back room. He realized that whoever had fired the shot had been standing in that dark room.

He snatched a lantern from the wall, dashed into the room. Except for a table and a couple of chairs, the room was empty. He set the lantern down on the table, went to the back of the room. He opened the door, stepped out into the alley. There was enough moonlight to light the area, but he saw nothing. He listened, didn't hear anyone running or riding away. He went to the corner of the building, looked down the narrow passageway. Again, nothing. He checked the other side of the building.

Bolt went back inside the small room, closed the door. He wished he had checked the room first. He might have stood a chance of catching the shooter.

As he walked back across the room, something alerted his senses. He smelled the acrid smell of gun powder, but there was something else, too. A flowery scent, mingled with the overpowering smell of the gun powder.

He tried to place the scent. Maybe from the coal oil lantern. Or candle wax from the candle that sat on the table.

Or a woman's perfume.

Chapter Sixteen

Tom and Hard Luck Hal were bent over Alexis when Bolt returned a few minutes later. Alexis was still unconscious. Hard Luck Hal moved away when Bolt stooped down.

Bolt ripped the bloodstained sleeve away from the wound. He leaned over, looked into the hole, felt the back of her arm, found an exit wound. The bullet had gone clean through the flesh part of her upper arm. Bolt couldn't tell if any bones were broken. He ripped a piece of cloth from her dress, tied it around her arm, just above the bullet wound. He took another piece of cloth, covered the hole, tied it in place.

"Anybody got a wagon?" Bolt asked. "We gotta get her to the doctor."

The men shook their heads.

"Doc Ackroyd is just down the street," Hard Luck Hal said. "We can carry her."

"There was a carriage across the street when I came in," offered one of the men. "Maybe we could borrow it to cart her down there."

"It would be easier," Bolt said. "I don't want to hurt her arm. Go check on it."

The man left, came back a minute later.

"Nope. It's gone. We just missed it. I saw it pulling around the corner."

"Alexis, Alexis, wake up," Bolt called. He patted her cheeks but got no response. "Looks like we carry her."

Bolt slipped his arms under her lithe body. He told Tom to hold her arm in place while he lifted her gently. He carried her through the throng of gawking men, out into the night.

Hard Luck Hal ran ahead, alerted Sam Ackroyd, the barber/surgeon, that they were coming. Several times, as they walked the long block, Tom took her legs, helped support her.

"Bring her on in," Ackroyd said as he greeted them at the door. He led them to a side room beyond the barber shop. "Put her down on the cot."

Alexis moaned when he set her down. Her eyes fluttered open. When she saw Bolt, she started to get up.

Bolt pushed her back down.

"You're all right, Alexis. Dock Ackroyd is going to take care of your arm."

"Bolt. I didn't tell you. Her name was Madge Garrett," Alexis said, her voice weak and soft.

"Thanks, Alexis. I had already figured it out but it's nice to know I was right."

Bolt stepped back to give the doctor working space.

Doc Ackroyd removed the emergency bandage and tourniquet from her arm, wiped the blood away from the wound with a sterile cloth. He checked the wound carefully, felt the exit wound with his fingers.

"Bullet went clean through the fleshy part of her arm," Doc Ackroyd announced. "She's lucky it didn't hit a bone. She'll be sore for a few days, but the damage won't be permanent."

"Glad to hear it," Bolt said.

"If you fellers want to wait in the other room, I'll clean the wound and wrap it with a fresh dressing. Take me about twenty minutes, then you can take her home.

With heads lowered, the three men filed from the room.

"She took your bullet, didn't she?" Tom asked when they were in the barber shop area of the house.

"Yes, damn it."

"They're out to fix your wagon tonight, ain't they?" Hard Luck Hal spouted. "You've got somethin' comin' at you every time you turn around."

"Yeah. I'm beginning to think I should have stayed in bed," Bolt smiled. "I think I've had about all the excitement I can stand for one night." He shook his head, collapsed in the comfortable barber chair.

"Think it was Rader who shot at you?" Tom asked.

"Hell, it could have been anybody," Bolt sighed. "Rader, the sheriff. Another hired gunny. Somebody who didn't like what I had to say at the meeting today. Who knows?"

"I think it was that thar sheriff what done it," Hard Luck Hal laughed. "Hell, the way you was pokin' fun at him tonight. Don't think he took a fancy to it."

The front door of the barber shop burst open. Dinger came in, out of breath.

"Been lookin' all over for you," he pouted. "Sybil's been kidnapped."

"What?" Bolt hopped down from the barber chair.

"It's true. Somebody carted her off through the winder."

"When?" Bolt asked.

"Forty, forty-five minutes ago. We just discovered she was missing a little while ago."

"Got any ideas who did it?"

"Nope. That's why I come lookin' fer you. Figured you'd know what to do. Want me to go fer the sheriff?"

"Hell, no," Hard Luck Hal snorted.

"No. I'll go right back with you." Bolt stuck his head in the other room, told Doc Ackroyd to keep Alexis until he got back.

At the bordello, Lucy and the other girls, the two miners, dashed up to Bolt.

"Oh, isn't it awful?" Lucy cried. "Poor Sybil. I can't believe this has happened."

"Did you see who did it?" Bolt asked.

"Yes. It was a man I'd never seen before. Nice, pleasant sort, ruggedly handsome. I didn't think to get his name. He paid for Sybil's services. They were up there a long time and when I went up to check on her, we discovered she was gone."

Bolt went up and checked the room, saw the knotted bed linens. He walked over to the window, looked down below, saw nothing but silver tips of the moonlit trees around that side of the house.

"Tom, grab a lantern," Bolt said when he was back downstairs. "I want to check outside."

Tom took a lantern from one of the tables, followed his friend outside.

Not wanting to miss any of the excitement, Hard

Luck Hal trotted along behind them.

Bolt went around to the side of the house, stood under Sybil's window, looked up. He figured the man who kidnapped her was not a big man because the empty bed wouldn't have been heavy enough to hold much weight without moving.

"Shine that on the ground, Tom."

"Find something?"

"There are two sets of hoof marks here, two horses. Whoever kidnapped Sybil wasn't working alone."

"Rader's work?" Tom asked.

"It's gotta be. At least he's giving the orders."

"Hope they ain't plannin' to tar and feather that gal again," Hark Luck Hal said.

"Naw," Tom said. "Ain't Rader's style to do that unless there's a big crowd around him so he can show off. He likes to play the big shot."

"Assuming Rader is responsible for Sybil's kidnapping," Bolt said, "we've got to figure out where he'd hide her out. I don't think he'd be dumb enough to take her home with him."

"Hell no," cackled Hard Luck Hal. "Madge would chop his balls off and feed 'em to him for supper if he ever brought another woman home."

"What about the Rader's store," Tom suggested.

"Naw," mumbled Hard Luck Hal.

"Pete Booker's place?"

"Or a house belonging to one of the Merchants Association members," Bolt said hopelessly.

"Naw. Too ordinary," said Hal, enjoying the excitement of the mystery.

"You're right," said Bolt. "It would have to be an out-of-the-way place. Do you know of any abandoned farm houses around here, Hal? A hoot owl shack? A hideout cabin?"

"A cabin. That's it," Hal cried. "Rader owns a hunting cabin out in the woods. But it shore ain't no hideout shack."

"You know where it is?"

"Shore I know. Not many do, though. I go pokin' all around these hills and you'd shit your britches if you knowd what I find. You want me to show you out to there?"

"Yeah. Tom, go by the doc's office and tell him to keep Alexis there overnight. Then do some checking around town. See if you can dig up anything. I'll go tell Lucy we're leaving."

Bolt went in and told Lucy that the three of them were going out looking for Sybil. Dinger and two other miners agreed to stay there at the bordello all night in case there was more trouble.

"That's it. Over there," Hard Luck Hal said when he saw the orange glow in the woods. They rode in a little closer, tied their horses to a pine tree.

Walking quietly, they snuck up to the house. Keeping their heads below the level of the window, they edged their way along the building until they reached the window where the light was glowing.

Bolt raised up slowly, peeked into the room. His jaw tightened as anger flared up in the pit of his stomach.

Inside the room, Sybil lay naked on the bed, spread-eagle, her wrists and ankles tied to the four bedposts. Sybil's head was turned away from the window, away from her attacker.

The rugged, muscular man standing next to the bed was naked to the waist. He had already removed his boots, hung his gunbelt on the bedpost.

Bolt's anger deepened as he watched the man begin to unbutton his trousers.

Bolt pulled Hard Luck Hal back away from the house where they could talk.

"Looks like we got here just in time," Bolt whispered.

"Yair. Why didn't you blow his balls off while you had the chance?"

"'Cause I don't shoot a man unless he draws first. That scoundrel isn't even wearing a gun. You stay here at the window and cover me. I'm going around front, see if I can surprise him.

As Bolt tiptoed away, Hard Luck Hal took up his post at the window. He popped his head up just high enough to be able to see inside.

The man had his back turned to the window as he pushed his trousers down his leg, tugged each pant leg off his feet.

The man turned sideways, tossed his trousers to a nearby chair. Next came the baggy shorts. The man stepped out of his shorts, was already bone hard.

Hal looked again, saw Sybil struggle against the cloth ropes that bound her.

The man positioned himself above her. Sybil struggled harder, cried out, "No!" She turned her head away from his kiss. The attacker lowered himself.

Hard Luck Hal leaned closer to the window, had an urge to sneeze. He jammed his finger against the bottom of his nose, tried to stifle the tickling itch.

He was too late. He tipped his head back, sneezed a sneeze loud enough to be heard by Bolt who was just going up the front steps.

The attacker froze, listened, jumped off the bed like a shot.

Hard Luck Hal watched as the attacker snatched his pistol from the gunbelt, spun the chamber, cocked the hammer back. The naked man ran from the room.

The last thing Hard Luck Hal saw of the man was his white bare ass.

Bolt had just stepped inside the brightly lit room when he heard the attacker jumping off the bed. He drew his pistol, pointed it at the doorway.

The man ran into the room, was halfway to the open door when he spotted Bolt.

"Don't shoot, mister," he shouted as he tossed the pistol to the floor, threw up his hands. Like a streak, he dashed out the open door, ran out into the darkness.

Bolt went to the door, saw the man disappear into the dark trees.

Hard Luck Hal saw the frightened man run by, his bare ass silvered by the moonlight. Hal fired a warning shot straight up in the air. It would be enough to guarantee the man didn't come back for seconds.

Bolt went on into the bedroom. When Sybil saw him, she shouted, began to cry.

"Oh, Bolt, you've done it again. You've saved my life."

"Don't count on me making a habit of it," Bolt grinned as he threw a blanket over her naked body and then began to untie her hands.

Hard Luck Hal walked into the room, smiled at

Sybil. "You all right?"

"Yes, I don't know how you found me, but I'm sure glad you did."

"Was easy once we put two and two together. I told you, Bolt, it pays to poke around these hills."

"Did you know who that man was, Sybil?" Bolt asked.

"No, he's new in town, I reckon."

"I knowd who he were the minute I saw him," Hard Luck Hal grinned.

"You did?" Bolt said, surprised. "Who is it?"

"It's that new kid what works for Calvin Rader. His name is Mac Cahn."

"I knew Rader was in on it," Bolt said as he finished untying her. "Get your clothes on, Sybil. We can't stay here."

"You going back to the whorehouse?" Hard Luck Hal asked.

"No, not tonight," Bolt said. "Might be trouble if Rader gets wind of this. I think it best if I hide her out for tonight."

"Well, you can't go back to your hotel room either. That's the first place Rader would look if Mac tells him we was here. I'll tell you what. You take the little lady down to my shack for the night. No way in hell Rader would look for you there."

"You got a point, Hal."

"My shack ain't much, but it's home. It's got a good feather mattress on the floor."

"You sure we won't be putting you out?"

"Oh, don't worry. I won't be there."

"Where are you going to spend the night?"

"Well, I've always wanted to stay in one of them big fancy hotel rooms. I thought we'd just switch places fo the night."

"You got yourself a deal, Hal. You sure as hel deserve it."

"I sure as hell do."

Chapter Seventeen

Hard Luck Hal left for town with Bolt's hotel key shortly after he had taken Bolt and Sybil to his tiny shack.

Sybil removed her shoes, sat on the feather mattress which rested on the floor. The only other furnishings in the shack were a small rickety table with tottering legs and a single hard back chair.

Bolt took off his boots, sat at the other end of the mattress, facing her. Black soot smudged the glass chimney but it gave off enough light to splash the sides of their faces with its warm glow.

"I never thought I'd be grateful for a little shack like this," Bolt said, "but it looks like a palace tonight."

"I know what you mean. I heard you had some trouble this morning with Dave Talbot."

"Was that this morning? It seems like a year ago. The day got worse as it went along. For both of us."

"Bolt, what's going to happen?"

"I don't know. Rader's running out of ammunition, but every time I think that way, he comes up with another surprise."

Bolt put his hands behind his head, leaned bac
against the wall and for the first time that day, was ab
to relax.

"You know, Bolt, I feel safer here than any place I'v
been in the past few days."

"I was just thinking the same thing. Odd, isn't it, tha
a ramshackle shack like this can be more comfortin
than a hotel room or a fancy house. I can see why Har
Luck Hal is so happy-go-lucky. He was mighty tickle
to be able to stay in a hotel."

"Looks like we're going to have to share the be
tonight." She looked directly into Bolt's eyes, watche
his reaction.

"I reckon so. I sure as hell don't feel like sleeping o
the hard ground. I mean, I do like luxury," he grinned
"And speaking of bed, I think we'd better turn in. Yo
ready?"

"Yes." Sybil scooted over on the bed to make roo
for Bolt. She lay back, put her head on one of th
pillows.

Bolt blew out the coal oil lamp, crawled in beside he
without taking his clothes off.

Unable to sleep after the trying day, they both la
still for a long time, staring at the dark crude roo
boards above them.

"Bolt, could I ask you a question?" she finally sai

"You just did," he kidded.

"Is it true that you never make love to prostitutes?

"Never have."

"That's too bad."

"Not for me." Bolt wanted Sybil very much. It wa
tough being so close. And yet, he remembered what h

ad seen through the cabin window. He had seen the xpression on her face when Mac Cahn had tried to ape her. He didn't want her to think he was taking dvantage of the situation by having his way with her.

He respected her and wouldn't take her just because he was there. If she were anything but a prostitute, he vouldn't hesitate making a move. It was odd, he hought, but he had always been that way. He treated he ladies like whores and the whores like ladies.

"I want you, Bolt," she said in a soft husk. "I've vanted you to make love to me since the first time I saw ou. You remember what you said at the meeting today bout everybody having the right to choose?"

"Yes."

"Well, in all my life, I have never had the right to hoose my bed partner. I have always had to sleep with he men who choose me, but I never got to choose for nyself. I want to be able to choose for myself. I want ou to be the first."

"You make it awful tempting." Bolt felt the heat that urged into his loins, felt his manhood begin to stiffen.

"That first night you were here, when you made love o Lucy, I wanted you so much I thought I would die. n fact, I had planned to sneak into your room that ight, but Lucy beat me to it."

"You little scamp. I knew you had heard us. In fact, couldn't get you out of my mind, thinking of you in he very next room."

He leaned over and kissed her full on the mouth. Her iss was warm and moist, inviting. His manhood hrobbed and hardened.

"Please, Bolt, please make me happy."

"You know what? I'm going to break my rule

tonight. You're going to be my first, too."

They stripped out of their clothes, came together lik
they had never been apart.

She was expert in her manipulations, a wild anima
when he penetrated her, a tender, undulating woma
when he stroked her. He felt, for the very first time
very complete with a woman, like they were one power
ful force moving in the same direction.

When his climax came, he didn't try to hold it back
He let it come naturally as if everything before in lif
had prepared them for that one glorious moment whe
the universe was theirs.

They were comfortable with each other when it wa
over as they lingered in each other's arms.

"I've heard that whores make the best lovers," h
said, "and now I know it's true. You are a very specia
person."

"Bolt, I've made a decision tonight. I'm going to qui
the business. I want always to make my own choice.

Calvin Rader didn't hear anything about all th
shootings the night before until after he got to work th
next day and talked to Pete Booker. When Madge ha
returned home, she had gone right to her room and h
didn't want to listen to her nag, so he hadn't asked her i
she had gone to the sheriff's office or if any action ha
been taken.

Pete told him about the things he had heard about
About the sheriff's attempt to arrest Bolt, about th
stranger in town who had egged Bolt into a fatal shoot
out, fatal for the stranger, not Bolt. He told him tha
some mysterious person had taken a shot at Bolt at th

174

aloon, that the bullet had missed and hit Alexis Townsend instead.

He told him about the kidnapping and that he had only learned this morning that Bolt had once again rescued Sybil.

Rader got sicker and sicker as each event was revealed to him. He was desperate now. His fastest gun, Dave Talbot was dead. The gunny Talbot had hired had arrived on time, only to be killed by Bolt. Rader didn't know anything about the mysterious shot that wounded the schoolmarm. That was none of his doing.

Rader knew he couldn't even depend on the sheriff to attempt another arrest. He'd give up now, but he had to win the respect of his wife. That was all that mattered to him.

Everyone else had failed. Rader would not. He would do the job himself.

"Pete, we're going to burn the place down tonight."

"The bordello?"

"Yes. We're going to get everyone in town to march against them. We'll set torches to the whole damned building."

"You can't do that, Calvin. You can't take innocent lives like that."

"I'll promise you one thing. No one will be killed. I've been going after the wrong thing, Pete. All this time I've been going after Lucy and her girls when all I wanted gone was the whorehouse itself. I'll make sure everyone is out of the house before we burn it. It will be gone forever and we'll never let anyone build another one in Angel's Camp."

*   *   *

175

It was almost noon on Saturday when Bolt and Sybil returned to the bordello. Hard Luck Hal had stopped at the bordello on his way to the hotel to tell Lucy and the girls that Sybil was safe.

He had also told Tom not to bother looking for her any more.

Bolt and Sybil had made love half the night and then slept late like they didn't have a care in the world.

The glitter gals, dressed in long day dresses, swarmed around them. Hugged and kissed and cried. The miners who had stayed the night shook Bolt's hand, slapped him on the back.

From her living quarters in the back, Lucy Tucker heard the racket, went to greet them.

Bolt saw her coming down the hall, a tall, dark, handsome man right behind her. It surprised him to see her coming from her living quarters with a man, since she wasn't the type to entertain like that. He knew he had been the first man she'd had in five years. In a way it made him proud. Maybe he had been the one who had been responsible for her change of attitude toward men. She didn't trust them before, didn't want to be sexually involved. It was good, though, that she could relate to a man now.

"Bolt, you've done it again," she said as she threw her arms around his neck, gave him a quick kiss on the lips. "You're amazing, truly remarkable."

"I had help. If it hadn't been for Hard Luck Hal, I would have drawn a blank. He knows this territory like the back of his hand."

Lucy gave Sybil a big hug.

"I'm so glad you weren't hurt, Sybil. It's so good to

have you back."

"I didn't come to stay."

"What do you mean?"

"I'm not going to be a whore anymore."

"Is something wrong? Is it because you're frightened?"

"No. I just learned that it was nice to have a choice about who I sleep with."

Lucy looked over at Bolt, a questioning look on her face. He winked.

"What are you going to do with yourself, then?" Lucy asked Sybil. "How are you going to earn a living?"

"I don't know yet. But I know the right opportunity will come along. I feel very sure of myself."

"Well, you can stay here until you find something else. Maybe I can pay you some for helping around the house."

"Thanks, Lucy. I'll have to stay for a while at least. I'm so excited about life now it's going to be a while before I can get my thinking straight." The other girls gathered around Sybil, took her over to the couches. They wanted to hear all about last night.

"Oh, Bolt, there's someone I want you to meet." She turned, brought the nice-looking man into the conversation. "This is Paul Tucker, my . . . uh, my husband. Paul, this is a friend of mine, Jared Bolt."

"Nice to meet you, Paul." Bolt shook his hand, liked his firm, sure handgrasp. "You've got a very special wife."

"That's what I'm trying to tell her," Paul laughed. "She tells me you're very special, too."

"I reckon I just happened along when she needed some help and I seem to have a knack for being at the right place at the wrong time."

"From what she tells me, I think you've helped Lucy more than you realize."

Bolt saw the look in Paul's eyes. He wondered just how much Lucy had told him.

"I have a message for you from Alexis Townsend," Lucy said. "She said to tell you, first, that she wanted to thank you for saving her life and second, she's at home now and would like to see you. A couple of the girls and I went to see her at the doctor's this morning and we took her home."

"I didn't save her life," Bolt laughed. "She saved mine. That bullet had my name on it and for a change, she was in the right place at the wrong time. I'm going over there now."

"Good. The girls and I thought it would be fun to have a party tonight. Invite the miners. Kind of a celebration for the way things turned out."

"It isn't over yet. You know that, don't you? Rader is pushed to the wall. He's either going to crack or he's going to give up. But until it happens, we won't know which."

"I realize that, but if he's going to accomplish his goal and close us down, then that's all the more reason to have a party before it's over with. Will you and Tom come?"

"We wouldn't miss it."

Paul excused himself, said he needed something in town. After he was gone, Lucy invited Bolt to her living room in the back of the house.

"I'm scared, Bolt."

"Because of Paul? He seems very nice."

"He is. That's the trouble. He's been out of prison two months now and I don't know how he found me but he said I was the only thing that mattered to him. He wants us to go back together, that that was all he thought about all those years. He says he hasn't had anything to drink since he's been out of prison, hasn't had a drink since that horrible night five years ago. But I just don't know."

"Did you tell him about us? About the other night?"

"Yes. I told him you had been the only man besides himself."

"How did he react?"

"I expected him to be mad, but he was very gentle with me. He took me in his arms and held me for a long time, said he was glad I had found at least a brief time of happiness. It felt so good, so natural, to be in his arms again. Oh, I wish I could make a decision."

"You will, when the time comes. Do you still love him?"

"Yes. I always have. But I'm frightened. Paul promised me he would never drink again, but he promised me that before. If I went back with him, I wouldn't have any guarantee that he would not drink again."

"There are no guarantees in life, Lucy. Only you can decide whether you want to live life with all its risks or merely exist in a state of fear."

"I don't know how you do it, Bolt. You're so sure of yourself."

"That's because I'm too dumb to worry about the

things that might happen to me. I just roll with the punches."

"Aren't you worried about what Calvin Rader might do?"

"Nope. I'm going to let Calvin do the worrying for me. No sense in both of us using up our brain supply."

Chapter Eighteen

Bolt stopped to see Alexis when he left Lucy's Place. She was resting on the couch, but feeling well. He told her about finding Sybil, left out some of the important details.

"Lucy's having a party tonight. She says it's either a farewell party or a celebration. Depends on Rader."

"Oh, I wish my arm was better. I'd love to go."

"You lost a lot of blood, Alexis. Now is not the time for you to be partying."

"What's a whorehouse look like? Inside I mean."

"Just like any other house, I reckon, decorated to suit the owner."

"But what about the rooms?"

"Well, they're somewhat smaller than the average size bedroom, but there are more of them. Usually upstairs if there is an upstairs."

"Do the girls really run around downstairs with very little on?"

"Sometimes. They usually wear the costume of their trade. Brief clothes that let a man know she's got a body, long silk stockings, painted faces, too much rouge, you know."

"I always think of a whorehouse as a place that's bright and gaudy. Pink and purple all over the place. Feathers and baubles. Pictures of nude women on the walls and perfume that stinks to high heaven."

"Each place is different. Some places are like you picture it. Others you wouldn't be able to tell from a boardinghouse or a family house. I'll tell you what I'll do. As soon as your arm is better, I'll take you on the grand tour of Lucy's, let you see for yourself."

"What's it like to be a . . . a whore?"

"Why? You interested in a job?" Bolt teased.

"No. I just wondered."

"That's one I can't answer. You'll have to ask one of the girls. I've got to get going. I'll check on you tomorrow."

"Don't forget your promise."

"I won't."

The hot damp towel felt good on Bolt's face. His eyes were closed, his head tipped back into the chair. He had already bathed and dressed in clean clothes for Lucy's party. He had come into the barber shop to pay Sam Ackroyd for patching Alexis up the night before and to get a two-bit shave. Sam whistled, sharpened the straight edge razor on a leather strap.

Bolt heard the barber shop door open.

"Howdy, Mort," Sam greeted. "Have a chair. I won't be long."

"I didn't come for a haircut," Mort Snyder said. "I'm just delivering messages for Calvin Rader."

182

Bolt's ears perked up. He did not move.

"Oh, what's up?" Mort said.

"Rader's planning a march on the bordello this evening so I'm letting everyone know."

"What time?"

"At sunset. Just at dusk."

"That's less than an hour from now. I don't know," Ackroyd said. "I may be busy with customers then."

"Oh, you won't have any customers. Rader said everyone in town is showing up. Those who don't go along with Rader's thinking are going along just to watch."

"Watch what?"

"Rader's going to torch the bordello tonight."

"Burn it down? No, I wouldn't go to such a display. I'm a doctor, after all. I save lives, not destroy them."

"Nobody'll get hurt. Rader plans to get everybody out first. He's just going to burn the building down so there won't be any more trouble over it."

"I don't like it, Mort."

"Some do. Some don't. But Rader's got enough men on his side that it doesn't make any difference. Even the sheriff is in agreement. He's deputized ten men in all just to make sure no one interferes."

"Well, count me out, Mort. I don't like mobs."

"I'm just delivering the message. I don't care one way or the other."

"Just see that you don't bring me any burn victims."

Bolt heard the door close, sat up in the chair and took the damp towel off his face.

"Rader's crazy," Sam said.

"He sure as hell is. Forget about the shave."

"Bolt, you ain't planning on stopping Rader, are

you? You heard what Mort said."

"Somebody has to," Bolt said as he dashed out the door, ran out to his horse, Nick. He rode across the street and down a few buildings to the hotel, ran upstairs and told Tom about the march. They ran down the stairs together and by the time they got outside, they saw the group beginning to form at the far end of the street. Calvin Rader was in the middle of the group, passing out unlit torches.

"Do what you can, Tom," Bolt called as he mounted his horse again.

"Aren't you going to the bordello?"

"No. I've got something that's more important." He rode off, left Tom totally baffled.

Bolt pushed Nick hard, arrived at the Rader ranch in less than fifteen minutes. Without bothering to tie Nick up, Bolt dashed up the steps, pounded on the door.

Madge opened the door a minute later. She gasped when she saw him.

"Bolt! What are you . . ."

He grabbed her arm, pulled her outside.

"Come on, you're going with me."

"Where? Why? I don't under . . ."

"We haven't got time. I'll explain later." He let her arm go.

"Well at least let me get my coat. It's cold outside."

"We don't have time. You can use mine."

"It's right here in the hall closet."

"Get it, then." Bolt stepped inside the entry hall while Madge walked five steps to the hall closet. Her scent lingered in her path, reached Bolt's nostrils. Something gnawed at his brain for recognition. As he watched her take her coat from the closet, he tried to figure it out. The smell, the perfume. That was it. Now he had the answer to one of his puzzles.

Madge closed the closet door, slipped into the coat. When she got to Bolt, he stepped in front of her, blocked her way.

"You fired the shot in the saloon last night," Bolt accused. "The one that wounded Alexis Townsend."

"I . . . uh . . ."

"Don't deny it, Madge. It's your perfume. The same perfume I smelled in that back room."

"Yes, I did it," she cried, relieved that she had been found out.

"All the time, I thought Alexis took my bullet. I thought someone was shooting at me. But, I was wrong. You aimed at Alexis, didn't you? You couldn't take the chance that she was going to tell me your maiden name. Isn't that right?"

"Yes."

"Well, you wasted your bullet. I had already figured you out. It took me some time, but I remembered your dream, your thrifty ways. Come on, now it's time to make amends."

It was dusk when they got back to town twenty minutes later. Bolt rode in on a side street, saw the throng approaching the bordello, flaming torches held high. He knew he was in time.

The torches blazed orange against the darkness of night. At least twenty of them with Calvin Rader leading the way. Sheriff Pettibone marched beside

Rader, carried a rifle instead of a torch. More than half of the town had turned out for the march. Most of them were spectators to the public display and stayed to the sides of the marching men.

Bolt halted his horse in the dark shadow of a cypress, paused for a moment to watch the marchers gather in front of Lucy's bordello with Calvin and the sheriff at the head of the crowd. He wanted Madge to witness her husband's part in the ceremony.

Tom Penrod stood alone at the top of the steps as the marchers closed rank, moved into the yard. Bolt touched spurs to Nick's flanks, rode around to the back of the bordello with his unwilling passenger.

"Lucy Tucker, come on out!" Rader shouted in loud clear words.

Penrod stepped forward, his hand just above his pistol.

"You got any messages for Lucy, you give 'em to me," he said boldly.

"You tell Lucy to get everybody out of the house, all them harlots included, cause we're gonna torch the place."

Tom turned, opened the front door a crack, spoke to someone in a voice that could not be heard by the noisy men. He closed the door, returned to his position on the porch.

"Nobody's coming out, Rader. We're calling your bluff."

Rader ignored Tom, called out again in a booming voice.

"Lucy! Get everyone out of the whorehouse! We're gonna burn it to the ground."

Tom started to draw his pistol slowly out of its

holster. Immediately a shot was fired straight up in the air by Sheriff Pettibone. Tom stepped back against the wall, moved to a dark corner of the porch.

"That's just a warning," Rader yelled. "Next time, you get nailed. Lucy, get them girls out here! You got two minutes. If you don't come out, we torch you anyway."

Lucy appeared in the front window. She opened it, called out to Rader.

"We're coming out. Wait till we're all outside."

Rader smiled to himself, puffed his chest out, smiled at the sheriff. He waited, counting the seconds off in his mime. When none of the girls had come one minute later, Rader called again.

"This is your last chance. The torches go down in thirty seconds."

"We're coming. Right now," Lucy called from the window.

The front door opened slowly. The crowd began to cheer. A minute later, the door burst open and Bolt stepped through it, with Madge Rader on his arm.

The crowd gasped. Rader's mouth fell open in shocked disbelief.

"Meet Madge Rader, folks," Bolt shouted, "once known as Madge Garrett. I know her well. She's one of the best little hookers in the business. She used to work for me at one of my whorehouses down in Tombstone. She made a lot of money, invested it wisely and finally quit the business. Now, if she can make good, why can't the girls here at Lucy's?"

The spectators looked at each other, couldn't believe what they were hearing.

"A lot of whores wind up marrying respectable

men," Bolt continued. "They make good wives. The
know how to keep a man from straying. And if the
don't, they know their men will be treated well at
respectable whorehouse. You call this stinkhole Angel'
Camp. Well, the only angels you got here are the one
in this house. The rest, aside from the schoolmarm, ar
all hypocrites. Now, back out of here. Put out thos
torches and get back to minding your own business
For those of you who want, Lucy's holding open hous
starting right now. There's plenty of food and drink
Lucy's guest of honor is Madge Garrett Rader who wil
answer any questions."

Madge opened her mouth to say something. Bol
smacked her on her buttocks with the flat of his hand
The crowd cheered.

"Dump your torches in the water trough and com
on in," Bolt said. He turned and took Madge back int
the large living room.

The crowd quickly filed beside the trough, droppe
their torches and went inside. Women who had alway
been curious to see inside of a whorehouse, followe
their husbands. They crowded around the harlots t
ask them questions while their husbands fought for ju
a look.

Lucy and her husband, Paul, rushed up to Bolt. Luc
threw her arms around his neck. Sybil Childs came u
from behind him, kissed him on the back of the nec

"You still interested in buying me out?" Lucy aske

"Why? You ready to sell?"

"Yes. Paul and I are going to move away fror
Angel's Camp, get a new start." Lucy looked up at he
husband, smiled. Paul wrapped his arm around he
waist, squeezed her.

188

Bolt turned to Sybil.

"Looks like I'm going to need a new manager, a madam. You interested?"

"With you for a boss, I'll do anything. Yes, I think I could learn to be a madam."

"Bolt, there's someone back in my living quarters who wants to see you," Lucy said.

"Who?"

"Go on back and find out."

Bolt walked back, opened the door to Lucy's private quarters. "Hi, Bolt, I couldn't wait for your private tour," Alexis Townsend said from the couch. "And neither could Peter." She turned and smiled at the man who had his arm around her.

"Will someone tell me what the hell's going on?" Bolt said. "Has everyone gone mad? You're the enemy, Pete."

"Not anymore," Alexis cooed. "Nothing wrong about being friendly neighbors, is there?"

"No, but . . ."

"Pete never did go along with Rader's thinking," Alexis explained. "I didn't know it until this morning. Pete came over to see how my arm was, but he apologized for something too. He was the one who saw you coming out of my house and reported to Rader. Pete and I discovered that we had the same views and Pete quit Rader, refused to go on the march."

"If you knew they were going to burn the place down, why would you risk being in here?"

"We knew you'd come along in time to save us," grinned Alexis.

Bolt slapped his hand to his forehead, turned and walked back to the crowd of people. Madge Rader dashed up to him, gave him a full kiss on the mouth.

"You were a pretty good gal, Madge. Why take it out on Lucy and her girls?"

"I was scared. Scared someone would know me. And I felt guilty."

"Well, do you think your past means much to these folks?"

"I guess not. I was a fool. Bolt, if you ever want to . . ."

"No, Madge. You know I never mess with the girls. Not even the ex-girls."

They hugged each other, turned around just in time to see Calvin pinch the buns of one of the girls. They both burst out laughing.

THE CONTINUING **SHELTER** SERIES
BY PAUL LEDD

#10: MASSACRE MOUNTAIN (972, $2.25)

A pistol-packin' lady suspects Shell is her enemy—and her gun isn't the only thing that goes off!

#11: RIO RAMPAGE (1141, $2.25)

Someone's put out a ten grand bounty on Shell's head. And it takes a wild ride down the raging rapids of the Rio Grande before Shell finds his man—and finds two songbirds in the bush as well!

#12: BLOOD MESA (1181, $2.25)

When Apaches close in around him, Shell thinks his vengeance trail is finally over. But he wakes up in the midst of a peaceful tribe so inclined toward sharing—that he sees no reason to decline the leader's daughter when she offers her bed!

#13: COMANCHERO BLOOD (1208, $2.25)

Shelter is heading straight into a Comanchero camp, where the meanest hombres in the West are waiting for him—with guns drawn. The only soft spot is Lita, a warm senorita whose brother is the leader of the Comanchero outlaws!